The Last Genie

Alec thought he'd heard the last from his old beer can where Abu the genie used to live. He'd only kept it for sentimental reasons, and now when he put it to his ear there was no longer any muttering or snoring like there had been when Abu was still in residence. And then, one day, there came from the hole at the top the strangest of sounds, a confused mixture of static and voices like the output of a cheap portable phone, and a cry for help. All the old memories come flooding back, and Alec finds his quiet life is disturbed once again . . .

Also available in Lions

The Last Genie

Robert Leeson

Lions
An Imprint of HarperCollins*Publishers*

First published in Great Britain in Lions 1993

Lions is an imprint of HarperCollins Children's Books,
a division of HarperCollins Publishers Ltd,
77/85 Fulham Palace Road, Hammersmith,
London W6 8JB

ISBN 0 00 674694-2

Set in Plantin
Printed and bound in Great Britain by
Cox & Wyman Ltd, Reading, Berks

It is written that the Earth rests upon the shoulders of a mighty Djinn, whose feet are planted on a massive rock. This, in turn, is poised on the horns of a gigantic bull, borne on the back of a stupendous fish – swimming for ever in the Sea of Eternity.

Deep, deep down, on the bed of that Sea, lies an endless Serpent, its coils winding seven times round the Nether World.

In the Serpent's jaws – its pillars like green teeth, dripping with verdigris, its arches and walls filmed with poisonous slime – sits the Palace of the Prince of Darkness.

And there, on this Day of Days, that which was to happen threw the Fate of the Seven Worlds and even of Time itself, into the balance.

Chapter One

Dahnash, Third Prince of Darkness, sat on his seat of livid bone in the heart of his palace, and brooded.

Dahnash was burly, but running to fat. His grandfather, Eiblis, the First Prince, had been renowned for his lean, satanic features. His father Rajmus, though less handsome, had still a sinister appeal.

But, in Dahnash, Evil had gone to the bad. Above his gross double chin and chubby cheeks peered out malevolent small eyes of a bilious green.

Eiblis, the First Far One, great mind and greater ego, had once rebelled against the Most High. For that he was cast out of the Upper World.

Rajmus, the Second Prince of Darkness, less intelligent, but still vainer, had joined with the King of the Sea in a second revolt against the forces of Truth and Light.

After a battle which almost, but not quite, destroyed the Seven Worlds, Rajmus and the King of the Sea were utterly defeated by Suleiman the Great.

The Forces of Evil, having lost two contests, now had to face the thought that if they rebelled again, and lost a third time, then the Universe would settle down to an everlasting time of Truth and Goodness.

The thought made Dahnash, Third Prince of all that is Evil, grind his teeth in fury.

From his father he had inherited a little intelligence, and a great deal of conceit. From his mother, daughter of the King of the Sea, he had inherited the vivid green curls which covered him from eyebrow to ankle.

Those who saw him for the first time gazed openmouthed. This he took as a sign of awe and his monstrous ego swelled even more.

Alas, when he was depressed, and thinking of the Triumph of Goodness and Truth depressed him enormously, his curls drooped and lay flat on his corpulence, till he looked like an amphibious orangutan.

At such moments, the Forces of Evil hid out of his sight in the oozing corridors of the Palace.

And this Day of Days was just such a day.

Open in front of Dahnash was a huge chest, its curving lid undulating with guardian serpents. Inside, however, was no glittering treasure, no gold or diamonds, but a massive lump of dull grey metal.

Yet to Dahnash, this was precious beyond belief. It was his life's work. Melted down in that shapeless ingot were all the magic lamps, rings, bottles ever given down the ages to fortunate men. These men had at their call mighty Djinns ready to do their bidding.

"What is thy will, O Master?" they would tell their owners. "Shall I serve you a heavenly meal, build you a mighty palace, bring you four and twenty gorgeous maidens, or destroy your enemies? Only command!"

Happy men. But for all that, one by one, they died. One by one their magic lamps, rings and bottles were laid aside, the secret dying with the owner.

And one by one they had come into the hands of Dahnash. His agents had gone from land to land, city to city, door to door, collecting them, for as little as possible. Dahnash was mean.

And in his quest, he was patient. His plan to have revenge for the defeat of his grandfather and father had taken so long. Now it was almost complete. Once all the metal was gathered in, all the Djinns of earth, air, fire and water would be his to command.

Then he would be ready to strike. Let the Forces of Truth and Light Beware – from Ibn Jann, King of Djinnistan, to Suleiman the Great, even to the Most High.

Dahnash was coming!

Fade from memory, O Eiblis. Be Forgotten, O Rajmus. In ages to come, you will be but a word in the Great Book of Perfidy. The Final Age of Evil, the Age of Dahnash, is about to dawn.

But with that great thought, the sea-green curls suddenly unrolled and hung on his limbs like seaweed on dank rock.

He had all the magic metal in the universe, all except twenty grammes of it, twenty cursed grammes, not enough to make a lamp or bottle, barely enough to make a ring. Hardly worth talking about.

Except – that it stood between him and control of the Spirit Beings of the Seven Worlds, between him and the unloosing of such a flood of unbearably deliciously vicious, vile, corrupt, dissolute and debauched Evil, that the mere thought of it made him almost pass out.

The pea-coloured hair stirred and wriggled across his skin for a moment, then lay still again. His heart was filled with gloom again.

"All I want," he gritted, "is to do enough Bad for the Ages to remember me. Is that too much to ask?"

For a split second his eyes rolled upwards as if he were about to beg some Higher Power for justice. Then he remembered where he was, and who he was, and shivered with the shame of it. There was no one in the entire world of worlds who could do more evil than he, Dahnash, and he was frustrated in this abysmal endeavour, by twenty unspeakable grammes of base metal, not worth the dirt from under a slave's fingernail.

It was too much.

He slammed shut the snake-girdled chest. Then he heard a cheerful whistling in the gloomy passage beyond. His head jerked up. Only one person would even dare move about the Palace when Dahnash was depressed. Certainly only one would dare whistle. He had a sneaking suspicion that it was a hymn tune as well, but did not know enough to be sure.

And here came the whistler, striding into the Throne Room with a jaunty step, lean, sea-green, mean and incredibly handsome – Jujuru, Dahnash's lieutenant and loyal servant.

Highly intelligent, Jujuru could have been diabolically dangerous, but he liked the easy, evil life. Most of his energy went in diverting his master from his most hare-brained schemes. Thus Jujuru was, in his way, a Great Force for Good – but he did not care to think too much about that.

Jujuru eased his bad conscience by encouraging Dahnash's insane dreams. Yet he knew that a Universe without Good was an utter impossibility, and certainly not to be desired by any self-respecting wrong-doer. Without Good, how did you know what you were doing was wicked? And how could you enjoy it?

Jujuru understood this. Dahnash did not. So for the sake of Evil, Jujuru had to do good.

"Greetings, O Prince of Depravity. O Lord of Debauchery!"

Dahnash sulked. The whistling still irritated him.

Jujuru was not discouraged. He bowed to his master's feet. With long practice he could do this standing up because he found it humiliating to get to his knees.

"Your slave has been about among the Children of Adam, encouraging them in sin and malefaction – although wickedness knows, they need no instruction from me – an evil lot."

"Shut your unbearably pompous mouth," snarled Dahnash.

"It is permitted," answered Jujuru respectfully,

then went on. "O Prince, live for ever, I bring tidings . . ."

"What tidings?"

"Good tidings, and . . ." Jujuru eyed his master.

"Tell me!" The hair began to stir.

"The last piece of metal is found."

"What? When? How? Where? Give it to me," Dahnash began to gibber in his excitement.

". . . and there are bad tidings," went on Jujuru, stepping to the side as Dahnash raised his arm. A thoughtlessly hurled lightning bolt could spoil one's complexion for days – and evil ones, like virtuous folk, are vain about their appearance.

"The metal is in a far country."

"Which?"

"Inghilterra. England."

"Go, then and get it."

Jujuru eyed his master warily.

"That will be difficult – perhaps impossible."

Dahnash swelled with bottled-up rage.

"You are telling me that after recovering masses of magic metal from the Seven Worlds, you will find it impossible to get hold of a mere twenty grammes, a ring, a trifle . . ."

Jujuru shook his head patiently.

"Not a ring, nor a lamp, nor a bottle, Most Eminent, but a can."

"A can?" Dahnash was baffled.

"A small vessel from which people drink once, then hurl from them in contempt. Every street in Inghilterra is littered with such things."

"O Stupid One!" Dahnash knew this was the only adjective which could hurt Jujuru. "Go there, find another can, exchange them secretly. Go!"

"Lord of Corruption, that may not be. One Law binds both Good and Evil. Magic metal may not be taken by force or stolen. The owner must be persuaded to give it up willingly."

"Then *persuade* him."

Again Jujuru shook his head. Dahnash ground his teeth until sparks flew from his lips.

"Master," went on Jujuru. "This owner is different from other owners. He treasures the can, in a special way."

Dahnash spluttered with derision.

"How can he? How can a small piece of magic metal have such value?"

Jujuru shrugged.

"The powers are small. The djinn it controls is a humble one, only of the Third Order and rank. His name is Abu Salem."

"So?"

"The owner cherishes the can because of his deep friendship and affection for the djinn."

Dahnash's eyes popped. "Friendship? Affection?" The words seemed to stick in his gullet, then he roared. "Are you telling me this master made a friend of his djinn, a third class djinn? What sort of man is this?"

"He is called Alec Bowden."

"Al Ek Bahdeen," Dahnash repeated, then laughed so hugely he fell backwards. "One who comes late."

13

Getting his breath back he demanded again: "What sort of man is that?"

"Not a man, O Prince of Darkness, but a boy."

Dahnash's voice went up the scale.

"A boy? A boy? Show me."

Jujuru bowed, then waved his hand. The two moved a few paces across the hall to a huge table hewn from a single piece of jade. Jujuru raised a hand. The top of the table clouded, then cleared to show a picture.

They were looking into a library. Rows of shelves lined with books stretched away on either side. And in front of one shelf, clutching an old, leather-bound volume, was a boy.

He was smallish, thin with fair hair and grey-brown eyes. A shirt, which had been white, hung open at his neck, loosely held by a half-knotted tie. The tail of the shirt showed above the top of his grey trousers. Lost to the world, he read intently.

"A boy?" jeered Dahnash. "Standing there head in a book when he should be out in the sunshine, kicking a smaller child, stealing its toys, wringing a sparrow's neck or tearing the wings from flies . . ."

"He is reading . . . about you," said Jujuru.

"About me?" Dahnash was flattered, then suspicious. "What about me?"

Jujuru sidled to the far side of the table.

"A story about your downfall."

Dahnash controlled himself: "So, all that stands between me and Lordship over the Seven Worlds, is a juvenile bookworm. And you say it's impossible?"

"O Lord of Infamy. I said that it may be impossible. But I believe I know a way."

"O infinitely clever Jujuru. Tell me, slave, if you are so brilliant, why am I your master?"

Jujuru bowed.

"If a master had servants more stupid than he, then nothing would work."

Dahnash's face convulsed as he tried to understand this. Then he gave up the attempt.

"Very well. How may we persuade this boy to give up his magic metal?"

"O Lord of Mischief. We convince the boy that his Djinn, his dear friend, Abu Salem, is in danger of destruction and that to save him, he must give up the can."

Now Dahnash's face radiated an evil joy. This sort of thing he understood.

"Splendid. Go to Djinnistan, secretly. Abduct Abu Salem, subject him to abominable torture. Better still, bring him here and I will do it. The boy will easily be persuaded to surrender his magic can, if this *friendship*," Dahnash spat out the word, "is what you say it is."

"Alas . . ."

"Alas? What do you mean – 'alas'? What are you hiding from me?"

"Alas, it is not I who is hiding anything. It is Abu Salem . . ."

"What? How?"

"He has vanished from the face of the Seven Worlds. Once it became known in Djinnistan that you lacked only one tiny piece of magic metal, Abu Salem, the djinn of the can, disappeared."

As Dahnash's face twisted in frustration, Jujuru pointed to the table image.

"The boy is the key. Convince him Abu Salem is in danger, lure him through time and space to Djinnistan and Ibn Jann, King of the Djinns, will be forced to reveal to him where Abu Salem is hidden."

"Forced to?"

"The Second Law which binds both Good and Evil: none may keep a master from his djinn slave if he seeks him."

"Aha. But will the boy rise to the bait?"

"We have a card to play, O Prince."

"What card?"

"Abdul, the son of Abu Salem."

"Abdul, son of Abu? Wait," murmured Dahnash. "That name rings bells in my memory."

"My master is wise beyond measure. This son of Abu Salem is known to us because he is wild, wayward and not entirely trustworthy. He likes to play games on the borders of Good and Evil. He and I have been," Jujuru spoke delicately, "in touch now and then. He may be *induced* to help us."

"Ah," said Dahnash.

Jujuru pointed to the image in the table top. The boy still stood absorbed in his book.

"Behold the last master of the last djinn. He has the power to change the history of the universe, the course of Time itself."

"Ha, he would not dare."

"We shall see what he will dare. One thing we can predict, Lord of Disgust, about the children of Adam, is that they are unpredictable. Alec Bowden knows neither the hour of the day nor the day of the week. But if we tell him he must make a great sacrifice to save Abu Salem, we shall see what he will dare."

Dahnash's chest swelled. The hair rolled into a mass of tight green curls. His voice roared through the fetid air of the throne room.

"Why wait? O Face of Ill Omen! Go and Do."

Jujuru bowed low: "Hearing is obeying, O Prince."

Then he was gone.

The words which passed between Dahnash and Jujuru, far beneath the Sea of Eternity, were heard through Seven Worlds. They reached the red-gold palace of Ibn Jann, King of Djinnistan, where he sat among his Grand Council, seeing to the Good of the Universe.

He shook his head.

"This cannot be allowed," he murmured.

The venerable Djinns around him shook their heads likewise.

"This may not be," they said.

An ancient Djinn spoke. "We must stop this Youth with his magic can, before he can be lured here."

But Ibn Jann shook his head once more.

"None may stop a master from seeking his servant Djinn."

All round the table nodded. This was true.

After a moment, Ibn Jann went on. "However, there is something we may do. We may distract him a little until another way becomes clear. And for this task, we will send . . ."

He turned and looked down the massed ranks of Djinns who packed the great pillared hall.

"We shall send – Maimunah."

There was an immediate chorus of alarm from the Elders.

"Maimunah – far too young!"

"So reckless!"

"So frivolous!"

"Maimunah? She's no more than a girl!"

"No more, no less," answered Ibn Jann. "We will send Maimunah."

Chapter Two

Alec was heading through the library on his way to the fantasy shelves when something made him stop and turn aside. He was hurrying to pick up the latest Terry Pratchett book before anyone else got their greedy paws on it. Normally nothing would have diverted him from such an errand.

But today something did.

It was as though someone had taken his arm and pulled him over to this shelf with its row of old books. Later he understood why it had happened but right at that moment it seemed like an impulse. He stopped at the shelf and picked out a book. There were more than a dozen, and on the outside they all looked the same – dull brown leather binding, faded gold lettering – the sort of book he never looked at. Until today.

Inside, the pages were frail, thin, almost transparent. He gingerly lifted one and a faded, once gaudy picture caught his eye. A giant, hairy figure, muscles swollen with power, ugly face made more hideous with rage, glared out.

The caption read: "Dahnash, Prince of Iniquity, reached out his foul hands towards the helpless victim."

Alec felt a shudder of fear. It came not from the sight of the picture but from deep inside his own thoughts. And in that moment another face came into his mind. It was a lined brown face, beneath a crumpled turban, a kindly smile, wise, humorous eyes.

Abu! Old Abu Salem, the Third Class Genie from Old Baghdad.

Now Alec held the book but no longer saw it. His thoughts flew back to last year and the fantastic things that happened when Abu Salem the genie had materialized from that old empty beer can.

The most fantastic thing was that he – Alec Bowden whose life usually swung between triumphs (now and then) and disasters (every day) – should have a genie with magic powers at his bidding.

Those magic meals they'd shared, the tricks they'd tried, those that went right, and more often, those that went wrong. Then one day Alec had asked him to do one piece of magic that was too much for him and he'd vanished again.

But then along came Abdul, Abu's son, nutty as they come, uncontrollable, causing fifty different sorts of chaos until the powers that be called him back.

What a time, like a dream! And now nothing more to show for it than that old can, scratched and dingy, sitting on a shelf over his bed.

Correction, there was something good left over from last year. He'd made friends with Ginger Wallace, and his sister, Eulalia.

Eulalia. She was something else. Alec felt his face turn red and quickly looked round to see if anyone was looking. Relieved, he turned back.

He came out of his trance with a jolt, stuck the old book back into its place and rushed to the fantasy shelves. Some unspeakable nerd had taken the latest Terry Pratchett book. Disasters one, triumphs nil, the story of my life, he thought.

Still brooding, he began to leave the library. But as he went past the shelves, the row of old books caught his eye again. Swiftly he lifted one down. It fell open at the same page, that awesome figure of Dahnash, the Far One, Prince of Evil.

He turned back to the beginning of the book and saw the title: *A Thousand and One Nights*. Of course, The Arabian Nights. He began rapidly to read, opening first one volume then another.

Hang about, where was the story of Aladdin and his Lamp, or Ali Baba and the Forty Thieves, or Sinbad the Sailor? Still, there were one . . . two . . . three . . . sixteen volumes. There really had been a thousand nights. This girl Shahrazad must have been telling stories non-stop for three years – until her crazy husband got tired of chopping women's heads off.

There were hundreds of stories, battles, armies

by the million, men, spirits, beasts. Heroes and heroines, women disguised as blokes in full armour, charging over the desert, running their lances through three enemies at once so that they were spitted like a shish kebab. "With one stroke of his blade he made two where there was one before."

And feasts – a thousand baked camels, two hundred roast chicken stuffed with pistachio nuts, almonds and raisins, pastries dripping with honey. Again he thought of Abu Salem and their meals together.

And tricks, capers, jokes and curses: "My finger in your eye, O Son of a Thousand Pigs."

Cramp in his foot (why was he standing on one leg?) made him stop reading. He looked at his watch. It was half past five already. Get moving, Bowden.

He wandered home, mind full of the stories, but whatever he thought of he came back to those two faces, the evil mug of Dahnash and the kindly smile of Abu Salem.

Still in a dream, he arrived home late for tea. His Mum's telling off went over his head. Sister Kim on a visit pulled his leg – as usual.

"Did you ever see a dream walking? You know what his trouble is – Eulalia Wallace. At his age they can't keep their minds off the opposite sex."

Alec ignored her. Didn't even turn red. Thoughts whirled in his head. Dahnash, Abu Salem. What was it all about? Last year, Abu told him: "I must leave you, for a long time." How long was long? And what made him look in those old books?

In his room that night he saw the old can on the shelf over the bed. He'd kept it for sentimental reasons. He didn't really expect Abu or Abdul his son to pop out, did he?

He picked up the can, light, empty, blew the dust from the top. Then, holding it to his lips, he whispered: "Salaam Aleikum, O Abu Salem. Keef Haalek? How are you, mate? Where are you?"

But the can stayed silent. No voices, no mutterings, not even the comfortable snoring sound that told him, in the past, that the old genie was in residence.

Replacing the can, he undressed and went to sleep. But immediately he plunged into a nightmare. He was alone in a cavern, pitch dark, noisome. On either side, writhing sounds chilled his blood. Then he heard a faint call:

"Help, O Alec. Help me."

It was Abu. He knew it was Abu. Disregarding the dark, the foul air, the ghastly slithering noises, he ran forward.

"Abu, mate. I'm coming."

"Help, O Alec." Now the voice was further off, the more he ran. Then he plunged into a great cleft in the cavern rock and fell down, down.

He woke sweating, Abu's voice still in his ear.

Next day, the dream still gripped him. He reached school in a daze.

"Hey, Alec."

23

Someone grabbed his arm. It was Ronnie Carter.

"Where were you? I spoke to you twice, and you didn't hear me."

"Tough," said Alec, hardly seeing Ronnie.

"Going on Sunday?"

"Sunday?" Alec stared.

"Yeah, the trip."

The trip? Alec remembered. The club outing to Blackpool, the illuminations, the pleasure beach, the white knuckles, the shouts, the screams, the laughs, and home in the small hours. Somehow that had gone out of his head.

Ronnie Carter nudged him.

"Going with you know who? Hey, Eu-know-who. Get it? Hey, Bowden, you'd forgotten, hadn't you? Wait till I tell her."

Alec moved off at high speed, leaving Ronnie Carter gawping. He *was* going with Eulalia on the trip. The first time they'd really dated – though there'd be thirty other people around. Still.

But that was the crazy thing. This Dahnash-Abu thing had driven it right out of his head.

Suppose Carter did tell her? Alec hurried into school. He must find Eulalia before that clown did. To his relief she was at her desk, laughing, chatting with two friends. They turned.

"Look who's there, Eu. Bowden the Beast."

"Knock it off," she told them severely. Then she grinned and waved to him.

"Hey, Alec," she called. "Don't forget . . . the club tonight."

24

"Sure," he answered, baffled. What was that for? Friday night was always club night.

"All right, Mr Bowden," called Mr Hitchen from the front of the class. "Stop pestering the ladies and sit down."

Alec sank down at his desk and tried to grapple with the day's work. But already he was back in his dream – Abu Salem, Dahnash . . . danger.

When school finished, his feet found their own way to the library, to the same set of shelves, the same books. One stood out, half an inch beyond the rest. He took it down, it fell open, as if by magic, at the same menacing picture. And as he gazed, he heard Abu's voice in his mind.

Something *was* wrong. Some disaster, involving him, was looming. But what, what?

He dropped the book, caught it, shoved it back in its place and ran full tilt from the library. He had just realised what the disaster was.

Taking the library steps three at a time, he slipped and fell onto the pavement. Bruised and winded, he picked himself up.

Bowden, you stupid plonker!

He must have spoken aloud. Two passing women looked at him in distaste. But he was off down the street, running like a maniac. The club! That was what Eulalia meant. The tickets for the outing, at the club, half past five. And it was quarter to six already.

Oh Bowden, Son of a Million Idiots.

The club door was open as he panted up. He was in time. But Ronnie Carter stood there, shaking his head.

"Save your breath, Bowden. You've had it. Last one sold."

"You're kidding," Alec burst out.

"Negative, I didn't get one either. All gone."

So why was Carter smirking! Alec pushed past him into the club. The Leader was in her office, putting papers away. She shook her head at him.

"Sorry, Alec. When you didn't turn up, I thought you'd changed your mind. There was a big last-minute rush. If it's any consolation, you weren't the only one who missed out."

She slammed a drawer shut.

"I did say, tickets available until five thirty. For cash."

Alec nodded. There was no point arguing. He left the club house. To his relief, Ronnie Carter had gone. He couldn't stand any more gloating. But why was Carter so smug – if he'd not got a ticket?

He wandered down the road, heading home. In the gutter an empty beer can caught his eye. He gave it a flying kick and gloomily watched as it bounded away.

Beer can. Abu. Ah, if only Abu were here now. He could manage a rotten little ticket, couldn't he? Or a quick trip on the bedroom rug to Blackpool. But where *was* Abu?

26

He halted on the canal bridge and stared down. The murky water and the growing dusk suited his mood.

"O Bowden. O Unhappy One," he muttered.

Close by someone giggled, then laughed full-throated.

He looked up, embarrassed, then saw a slim girl in jeans perched on the parapet. Her handsome brown face was creased in merriment, white teeth showing.

"First sign of madness, Skinny. Talking to yourself."

She slipped from the wall and stepped up to him. Taller than him, her chin rested on his head, while her fingers tugged gently at his tie.

"You're in a bad mood, aren't you, Skinny?"

The nickname irritated him, even if it were true, though he didn't mind Eulalia using it.

"Aren't you looking forward to the trip on Sunday, eh?" she asked.

He looked at her. The dusk made it difficult to tell if she were mocking him or not. Did she know?

"Didn't get a ticket, did I?" He looked down at her fingers. She gently tugged on his tie again.

"Didn't get a ticket? I don't believe you. When I didn't see you there, I guessed you were first in the queue and had gone." Her voice sounded disappointed. But why was she smiling? Why did everyone think his disaster was so funny?

"I thought we had a date. We were going to sit together, weren't we? And you forgot to get a ticket. What's a girl to do? It makes one lose confidence."

This was humiliating. O Son of Shame!

Alec tried to twist away, but Eulalia held on to his tie.

"Don't you run away, Alec Bowden. I am really, truly, deeply annoyed with you. I am offended. Who is the other girl – somebody in the library?"

Alec gave a guilty start. Did she realise that when he should have been getting the ticket he'd had his head stuck in The Arabian Nights?

"I'm sorry, Eu. I just got there too late. Someone bought the last two tickets. Honest. They shouldn't really let people have two, should they?"

She laughed and laughed, letting go of his tie. Then, taking his arm, she began to walk him down the road.

"At the very least you can see me home, though it's going to take me some time to get over this. It hurts a girl's pride."

Suddenly she stopped and faced him.

"Oh Alec, love. You know who got the last two tickets?"

She shook him gently. "I did."

"You did?" Alec shouted.

"Shut up. I waited around to see if you'd come. Then when all the tickets were sold but two, and that Ronnie Carter turned up, I thought to myself – Alec Bowden, you do not have the sense you were born with, you are a total wa . . . wet week," she finished more kindly. "So I bought both tickets."

"Hey, that's great, Eu. Look. I've got the money with me. I'll let you have . . ."

"No you won't," she gave him another shake. "You get the ticket and you pay me Sunday – on the coach, when you turn up, ten a.m. absolute latest, in the Station Yard."

"No problem. I'll be there. Don't worry."

"You better, Bowden, 'cause I'll tell you what. Ronnie Carter asked me for that second ticket, so I told him he could have it if you turned up late."

"I won't be late."

"No, Skinny, you won't, not by one second. Or else."

Alec went home in high spirits. O Day of Gold, O Bright Bright Day.

He patiently endured the ticking off from Mum for being late for supper. Kim his sister was home on a visit, and he patiently endured her sarky remarks. She knew where he'd been and who he'd been with. He took it all in a spirit of calm, tolerant good will. Nothing could spoil his mood. Saturday went slowly. It was always like that when you were looking forward to something. In the morning he couldn't escape doing odd jobs for Mum. In the afternoon he had a sudden inspiration and slid round to the library. Guess what? It was closed. But at last the day ended.

That night, he fell asleep as his head touched the pillow. And before long he travelled into a chain of bizarre, exciting and alarming dreams, of deserts, caverns, monsters and undersea kingdoms.

He was cornered in a deep pit by an enormous scorpion which held him in its claws while the huge brown glistening tail, dripping venom, arched over to strike him dead.

Then the scorpion was flung to one side and torn to pieces by a gigantic ape with the face of a man.

"Come, O Alec, Abu Salem awaits you," growled the ape and rushed him through a labyrinth of rock passages.

On they sped. The passage grew narrower. Now they struggled through a cleft in the rock whose sharp edges pressed in closer and closer.

"Aaargh," gasped Alec, striking out with hands and feet.

And he was awake, half out of bed. It was broad daylight. The sun streamed in through his bedroom window, out of a bright blue sky.

Sunday morning. O Day of Destiny.

He wasn't going to be chewed by a scorpion, crushed by rocks. He was going on the trip with Eu . . . he was . . .

His eye, half open, fell on the battered alarm clock by his bed. It couldn't be. It must have stopped last night.

But no. He could hear it ticking.

It was five to ten.

Chapter Three

Alec rubbed the sleep from his bleary eyes with one hand, grabbed for the clock and shook it with the other, while kicking loose from the bedclothes with his feet.

For several seconds he struggled. Something had to give. Then he left the bed head first and landed sprawling on the floor, one toe still hooked in the sheet, while the clock, clutched in one hand, struck his nose and rolled out of his grasp.

Yet it still ticked. He didn't believe it. But a glance at his watch told him. That *was* the time. Only now it was four minutes to ten.

O Evil Day. Unlucky Bowden.

Scrambling to his feet, he lurched forward, slamming the clock back on the shelf. No point in arguing with it any more. What to do first? Wash, breakfast, dress? No, eating and washing were out. They were luxuries. Only dressing was essential. The feet of Time marched onwards, tick, tick, tick.

Dress, that was it. Shirt, jeans, socks, underpants, trainers. In what order? His brain, lagging several seconds behind his body tried desperately to take charge. Shirt on, over head, arms through sleeve holes.

No Bowden. Son of Stupidity. Get your pyjamas off first. Falling back on the bed he began to struggle with them. Unfastening buttons seemed too complicated. Was he awake? Pull the top over the head. Like that. His knuckles struck the shelf over the headboard. A shower of small change cascaded down his neck and slid into his pyjama trousers.

At the same time, the famous can tumbled from the shelf and rolled across the floor, making cronking noises. Reaching down, he snatched it up and was about to bang it back on to the shelf when he stopped rigid with amazement.

From the hole in the top of the can came the strangest of sounds, a confused mixture of static and voices like the output of a cheap portable phone.

Unthinking, he held the can to his ear. Time, place, everything else were forgotten. He was back one year in his life, listening to the voice of Abu Salem, Third Class Genie from the Court of Old Baghdad.

Only this time there was no deep reassuring bass voice – "What is thy will, O Alec?"

Through the crackling and tumult of voices came a breathless, strangled, "Help, O Alec, save thy humble slave from destruction. Help, before it is too late."

His eye blankly caught the slow circling of the second hand on his watch. Three minutes to ten. Down at the Station Yard people would be climbing up the steps of the coach, pushing, shoving, laughing, joking, while the leader called out the names . . . "Bowden, where's Bowden?"

But he could not move. The shirt hung loose from his left hand, his right hand jammed the can so hard to his ear that it cut into the soft skin.

"Help, O Alec! Do not abandon me!"

Alec's voice, husky with excitement and alarm answered.

"Abu. It's Alec. What's wrong? Where are you? What's happening? What are they doing to you? Your voice, it sounds weird."

Then from the jumble of static came another voice, lighter, yet urgent and commanding.

"Do not listen, Al-ec. This is deception. Your life will be in danger if you listen."

Abu again: "O Alec, there is little time left, an hour only, then I shall die in torment. I shall be utterly destroyed. My life is in your hands."

The other voice: "Do not listen. This is a dream. Stay where you are, live your life. Go to your friends, enjoy what you have. Do not risk all for a foolish fantasy . . ."

Suddenly a third voice joined the babble, lower but more urgent still.

"Friends, life, what are these words, if you betray him? O Unlucky Abu Salem, who served faithfully and was abandoned by a selfish master."

Then, more softly, like an echo:

"O Selfish Master. O Unlucky Day. O Cruel World."

"Help, O Alec!"

"Beware!"

"Come quickly!"

The voices ebbed and flowed, running through his mind while his glazed eyes stared fascinated at the circling second hand on his watch.

Now it was one minute to ten. He could see them filling the coach, hear the Leader calling:

"All right, Ronnie. If Alec's not coming, lad, on you get."

There was Eulalia, shifting along the seat to make room for the smirking Ronald. The driver was switching on the engine. Someone was singing: "Here we go, Here we go, Here we go."

Trapped by indecision, alarm and fear for his old friend Abu, confusion and disbelief he struggled to gather his wits – Is this happening to me: Is this You, O Alec, Unlucky Son of Worthy Parents?

The second hand counted down remorselessly: twenty-five, twenty-four, twenty-three. The coach was leaving, Abu's life was ticking away. Must do something.

"Shut up all of you," he yelled into the mouth of the can.

The babel of voices ceased suddenly. Alec spoke, tension making his voice rise up the scale.

"Somebody tell me. What do I have to do? I'll do anything I can to save Abu. But what, how, where do I go?"

There was no answer

"Tell me," he demanded again.

There was only silence. Rage filled him. Someone was making a monkey of him. Or he was going round the twist. Had he imagined it all – Abu, the threat to his life, the other voices pleading and warning? Was it all a dream? Would he wake up? No, he was awake all right. He'd missed the coach. His date with Eu was down the tube. She wouldn't laugh this time round. He'd had it.

O Day of Gloom. Ill-fated Bowden.

The second hand closed lovingly on the minute hand at the top of the watch dial. Ten o'clock. The coach was away down the Manchester road and he was lying on his bed, in his pyjamas, clutching his stupid can.

But something else was happening.

As the second hand passed the minute hand, the bed, with Alec on it, rose in the air, hung suspended for a brief instant, then flew towards the wall at a sickening rate. Before the impact, Alec threw up his hands to guard his face. The window rushed at him, then everything dissolved ahead and he was out in the clear autumn air.

Chapter Four

Petrified with fear and dizziness, Alec watched as his home, street, town gradually fell away beneath him, smaller and more distant by the second.

The estate was now a red-grey blob, the railway line a dark groove. Forcing himself to open his eyes, clutching the headboard with one hand and the can with the other, he stared downwards at the station and the yard where the club outing coach should be parked. It was empty except for a few cars. They'd gone – off to the sea. And he was going – in the opposite direction.

Then he realized that his legs were hanging over the side. A sudden swerve would shoot him off. Holding his breath, he inched his body into the centre of the bed.

Then came an inspiration. Cautiously pushing back the bedclothes, he slid beneath them and stuffed the pillows up against the headboard. Suddenly all the cold fear in his stomach melted away. He was sitting up in bed, as though he were convalescent, waiting for someone to come in with his breakfast. All his muscles relaxed. His skin warmed up, he wriggled arms and legs under the covers, grinned to himself and began carefully to look about him, forward, sideways, downwards. He was beginning to enjoy the ride.

As far as he could judge he was heading south. The bed seemed to know the way. The Pennines, brown and green, stained with the red of bracken, stretched away in front. Away on the right, to the west, he could make out the Wirral jutting rudely into the Irish Sea and the huge curve of Cardigan Bay. To the east was Norfolk, like a head bending over. That massive white-grey sprawl must be Birmingham. And the funny thing was, it all looked like a map. How high was he? He couldn't say. The air rushing past his cheeks was cold, but tucked up like this the rest of his body was warm.

That must be London ahead on the port bow (or was it starboard?). A gigantic mass of streets, railways, the spiral of flyovers, parks, tower blocks. As he grew more fascinated by what he could see, the bed slowed its flight and began slowly to descend.

But, even as it did, the can in his hand quivered and jumped. He clamped it to his ear. It filled with static, jumbled voices, squeaks and buzzes, then cleared to the strange half-strangled tones of Abu Salem.

"O Alec, Master of Goodness. Do not desert me. Save me from destruction."

"All right, all right, Abu, I'm on my way. Just hold on. I'll be there in," he thought rapidly, "just two shakes of a camel's doodle."

As he spoke, the bed tilted back, throwing him against the headboard, the foot rose and the whole strange craft began to accelerate like a rocket into the blue yonder criss-crossed with the vapour trials which he guessed must be from planes taking off from Heathrow and Gatwick.

A great shadow passed over him, followed by a powerful blast of wind. Just before it vanished, he saw the tail and blazing jets of an airliner. Suddenly his stomach went cold again. Should he have filed his flight plan? You could get stuck in the nick for not doing that. Still, too late to bother now.

Daring once more, he looked over the side. Much higher now, yet the air was so clear that he could make white cliffs, brown beaches and the creamy curl of waves on the shore out far, far below. He was over the Channel and heading for France.

The can crackled. He could hear voices again. But not Abu – English public school rather than Baghdad street-wise.

Alongside him, so close that he could see through the portholes, was a British Airways jet. Passengers' faces, white, alarmed, excited, glared out. Some were pointing video cameras. He chuckled. This must be a sensation on the 10.05 departure for Palma.

Now he could hear the captain's reassuring voice:

"Ha ha. I expect some of you will have noticed the bed over on our left side, just beyond the wing tip – fortunately. I'm just checking with control.

Probably some sort of publicity stunt for a rival airline. Ha ha. We're crossing the French coast now and still heading south south east . . ."

Water disappeared behind him. Now it was land, land, land, north, south, east, west. Alec lost his sense of which was which. The bed knew the way. The excitement of take-off was having its effect. He begun to nod off. As he felt his eyelids droop, he had the presence of mind to slide the can beneath the sheets. He was asleep.

He woke again to brilliant sun. A great tangle of dark mountains was sliding away under the bed and in front of him sparkling blue, endless blue in front of him, was the sea.

At the same time, he realized that the bed was slowing and losing height. That must be Italy down to the east. It really was like an old boot kicking Sicily – which was shaped like a potato crisp.

Down, down, down. That was Etna, wasn't it? Quiet in the sun, only wispy clouds curling up. And beyond in the ultramarine, a gaunt grey shape, flat-topped. Puzzled, he stared, then guessed. Hey, an aircraft carrier . . . US Sixth Fleet!

Any doubts were soon blown away as the can shook under the bedclothes. Snatching it out, he held it away from his ear as a formidable burst of static blasted out.

"Bed at three o'clock, ten thousand feet and coming in fast. Identify, identify . . .

"No code available. Hello, hello. Bed, are you receiving me? Give your identification code . . .

"Say, what is that? Nothing in the manual, sir. Zilch. Russian? Negative. Check with base, will ya?

"Say, aero-bed. That's like the Ay-rabian Nights? You don't say. That's Gadaffi. Saddam. Hey! Scramble, scramble! Bandits at eight thousand. Scramble, scramble."

Alec saw the black figures run like ants across the carrier deck below. The lean shapes jerking away from the ship.

Suddenly he realized his own danger. His stomach-curdling fear acted like a jet on the bed. Up, up and away it went at sickening speed. Alec, pressed flat by the acceleration, gritted his teeth and clung on, elbows pressed painfully into his side.

Now he was up beyond the top cloud layer. Below was an endless white world, so solid it seemed as though he could get out and walk on it. And above, the blinding blue white of the heavens.

And little white bursting clouds, turning red and black. Hey, what were those?

The delayed explosions told him. They were firing at him.

"Hey, you guys. Lay off," he screamed into the can. "I'm friendly. At least I was. Stop it, you maniacs. I'm just a ordinary guy on a mercy mission."

No one answered. The white-black-red bursts moved in closer. They were getting the range.

The bed suddenly changed course, south, and picked up speed. Now Alec pressed his eyes tight shut, slid right down into the bed and tried to retract his head into his shoulders, while the wind whistled past him like a storm.

Then it was quiet and calm again. Timidly he raised the can. The voices, the static had died down. Now all around him was grey fog. He was coming down through the cloud belt. The fog scattered, became wispier. Shots of sunlight blazed into his eyes and then he was in clear air again.

Below was another world. A dazzling world that caught the sun's rays and threw them upwards again, a world without limit – brown, orange-red, purple, splashes of green, then more reaches of yellow, gold, silver. This, thought Alec, in wonder, must be the Sahara.

Raising the can he called, "Hey, Abu. Soon be with you."

But there was no answer. The bed was changing course again, westwards. Where was he going now? It was the Atlantic that way, wasn't it – if you went far enough?

He sat up. The air was warm. He made himself comfortable again, back to the headboard. He looked around him below. Sand, sand, rock, sand, rock, sand as far as you could see – worse than Southport with the tide out.

Then he stopped, hand shading his eyes from the sun, and stared in disbelief at the horizon.

Right across his flight path, coming in fast from the south east, was an unidentified flying object. It wasn't a plane, though it was as big. And it wasn't a bird, though it came on wings, spread out graceful and menacing against the skyline. It was – he didn't believe it. It was impossible.

What was unbelievable was that as the creature came in closer – and it was homing in on him like a very, very intelligent bird of prey – it grew gradually smaller.

It was this thought that held him back from trying evasive action, although a mixture of apprehension and extreme curiosity held him rigid as it came closer and closer.

Now, at twenty feet, he could see it clearly, beyond a shadow of doubt. It was a girl of his own age, long and slim, with great wings which she slowly, lazily, began to fold as she approached – twenty, fifteen, ten feet. She wore multiple layers of flowing transparent garments, chemise, trousers, gold curling slippers and a fluttering white veil above which showed wickedly smiling eyes, brown, grey, blue, green, he couldn't tell because they changed with every second.

His mouth fell open. He tried to speak but his voice disappeared into his chest as the apparition folded her wings into herself so that they vanished completely, and landed with the lightest of thumps on the pillow beside him.

Chapter Five

Alec squinted sideways, taking the full force of those multi-coloured eyes. Strangely he didn't feel embarrassed. Today had already broken all rules, so . . .

She spoke, a deep, throaty voice.

"SabaaH Ilkheer. Morning of Goodness."

Without thinking, Alec replied:

"SabaaH Innur. Morning of Light."

She stared at him a second, then laughed. But it was not mocking.

"O Son of Worthy Parents. What is your name?"

"Alec Bowden."

She repeated the name in a way that made it sound bizarre, then laughed again. This time she was laughing at him. What was so funny? It was perfectly normal name.

"Why do you laugh?" he demanded, peeved.

"I will not tell you, yet."

Suit yourself. Alec racked his brains for a brilliant remark but could only think of: "What do they call you, O . . ."

She bent towards him and the veil floated out to tickle his nose.

"Your servant's name is Maimuñah."

Maimunah? He knew that name but couldn't think how. It must have sounded amid that jumble of static from the can. He had a vague feeling of unease, as though this girl might be bad news.

Lying there, so close that she almost touched him, made him think suddenly and guiltily of Eulalia. Then he thrust the thought from him. Eu was rubbing elbows with that rat Carter, wasn't she – just to teach Bowden a lesson. Well, two could play that game. A wave of recklessness swept through him.

"A second rising of the sun, this day. Will you show me your face?"

Behind the veil he heard her click her teeth.

"What if my lord's wives should return and find us here together?"

Alec gulped. He started to say, "I haven't got a wife," then impulsively changed it to "My wife is on a journey, to the sea, with another man, O Queen of Loveliness."

"Ah. Unhappy Al Ek."

She pulled lightly at the veil. It swung away to reveal a face that was at once brown and gold, mixing Chinese, Indian, African, high cheekbones, hooked nose, slant eyes.

"A man of such beauty should not travel alone." She bent over him, took his hand and gently began to remove the can.

At once Alec's doubts surged again. He jerked the hand away and stuffed the can under the pillow, then boldly reached out. But this time Maimunah made a face at him and said:

44

"This is no place for us to pass the time, you and I." She pointed down. "Below is my Palace of Delights. Let us go."

And immediately the bed dipped down and began to nosedive towards the desert below, sending the wind whistling past and Alec's stomach up into his throat.

But Maimunah only laughed. She seemed to be in control and at her urging the bed accelerated until the wind screamed in his ears.

Below them a green blob on the red-brown surface grew by the second into a ring of palm and olive trees circling a pool that sparkled blue in the sun. The sun's rays shone on a low white building with steps, arches and columns.

With a thump they had landed at the front of the palace. From the air it had seemed no bigger than a cricket pavilion. Now it looked enormous. A flight of twenty marble steps swept upwards to a great arched doorway.

Maimunah sprang lightly from the bed and held out her hand to Alec. Gripping the can, he struggled from the bedclothes and stood there, foolishly, in his pyjamas, gawping at what he saw.

A double line of figures, white, black, brown, yellow, women on one side dressed like Maimunah, men on the other stripped to the waist, brawny arms folded, huge gleaming scimitars in their belts.

As one they bowed from the waist. Alec, remembering he was in his pyjamas, was suddenly embarrassed, then reflected that no one else seemed to bother, pulled himself together and, hand in hand with the girl, advanced through the double line of slaves who were now crouched upon the ground.

"Long may you live, O Lord of Light," they chorused. As they passed from the heat of the day into the cool dusk of the hall beyond, he heard the splash of fountains in the gloom and stringed instruments playing softly behind curtains.

Then he remembered the bed. Whatever happened, he had to make sure he didn't lose sight of that, and the can. They were his means of escape if things screwed up and his only means of finding and rescuing Abu.

To his relief he saw four of the slaves carry the bed into the hall. From behind the curtains he heard light laughter and whispering.

"What are they saying?" he asked Maimunah.

"They have heard of the Prince with the Flying Horse but not the one with the Flying Bed," she chuckled.

Beyond the hall were more passages, room into room into room. Within a minute Alec had completely lost his sense of direction. And as they moved further into the palace, the sound of music and the scent of flowers, fruit and incense began to make his head spin.

Now they were in a chamber larger than the rest. An enormous carpet covered the floor and in its centre sat the biggest bed Alec had ever seen, draped with gauze and piled high with cushions of every colour.

Maimunah waved her hand. Alec guessed her

meaning and sat down. She sat down a little way away from him, and clapped her hands. In rushed more slaves, carrying gold jugs and bowls.

Before he knew it, they were washing him in rose water. It beat bath night in Bugletown any day of the week, but it was a bit alarming. He was relieved when they settled for a light sloosh and then retired bowing and giggling. Why was he so funny – was it the name? The face? The can? The bed?

Suddenly his nose caught the whiff of food – a hundred varieties. He was ravenous. And in they came, carrying dish after dish. Not like the small-scale feasts old Abu used to lay on in the hideout at home, more like the Arabian Nights themselves. This Maimunah was no Third Class Genie. She must be Division One. But she was so young – hardly older than him. What was she up to?

Hours passed, dishes came and went. Musicians played, girls danced. A male slave recited a long poem, which Alec did not understand, but judging by the laughter, it must have been a shaggy dog story – a dirty dog as well.

He was just beginning to realize that he was out of his league, when more slaves appeared with lamps. Outside, he saw that night had fallen. Maimunah rose.

"It is time for rest, my lord."

Alec yawned hugely. He was jet-lagged, he thought. His head spun.

"I must have my own bed, if I am to sleep properly."

She bowed. "As my lord pleases. But he will not fly away in the night?"

He shook his head. Where would he go?

More slaves led him to another room where his bed, now decorated with swathes of silk, stood. There was more whispering and tittering, then, finally, he was left alone.

His last recollection was of a gentle hand stealing under the pillows and searching round. But, lucky Bowden, he had removed the can and had it clutched to his middle. They wouldn't look there, would they? And he was asleep, in a deep dreamless sleep.

"O Emir of Excellence. It is morning. The time for ablutions."

Alec struggled out of bed. Light streamed from the shapely arched windows. On either side a line of slaves stretched to the farther door. Two stood by to help him from the bed.

"Make way for Al Ek Ba-Deen."

The passages resounded. Drawing himself up, Alec tried to look majestic. It was hard because they all seemed to be laughing at his name. But all the same, they were bowing and scraping. He marched forward.

The sun outside, light and heat, hit him in the face. From all sides came the girls who had greeted him yesterday. The male slaves he could see at a greater distance, standing blades drawn and held aloft between the palm trees that circled the pool.

Twenty pairs of hands seized him at once. He

was helped, urged, carried, rushed to the pool. More hands whipped off his pyjamas before he could blink. How he held on to the can was a miracle, but he did. Stripped, it was all he had left of home.

Then with a tremendous splash and twenty shrieks, he was in the water, choking, spluttering and laughing as they patted, pinched, pulled and poured water over him. It was like a session in the baths with the 4H hockey team – not that Alec had ever had one, but his imagination filled the gap. And he enjoyed it, he did.

Hours seemed to pass like minutes, then they were pulling him on to stone steps warmed by the sun, dabbing him with towels, spraying him with scent and rose water and, as always, tittering and whispering.

He could understand odd remarks.

"Oh, he is small and thin. No, you are a girl of no taste. He is slim, slim as the letter Alif, and fair. Those grey-brown eyes make my head whirl . . . If I could have him for an hour – Ha, the Lady Maimunah will boil you in oil."

The day dreamed away, more eating, more music. Maimunah was nowhere to be seen, though by evening the chatter around him had hushed and she came through the arches, tall and dazzling, to sit down by him, her eyes roguish.

There was only one way out. Alec let his head fall on his chest and began to snore gently. He heard her hands slap together sharply. Other arms lifted him up and slid him smoothly into his bed. Eyes closed, he began to breathe slowly and deeply. This time the probing hands returned under the sheets. They were looking for the can in the bed.

His breath left his lungs and climbed in a long thin squeak to his nostrils. How was he going to stop shrieking or bursting into laughter? Aaaaagh. There was only one remedy. He turned restlessly on his stomach, worked his hand sideways and tucked the can under the mattress. The hands moved away, disappeared and he was left to sleep, which he did, soundly.

And next morning came the light, the sun, the respectful greeting, the double line of slaves, the crowd of chuckling girls and the morning bath.

But as they dried him, there was something different. There was the usual sniggering and whispering. But someone spoke almost inaudibly but directly into his ear.

"Your slave Orange Blossom warns you. Today is the third day. My lady's good humour will not last for ever. She will have what she will have. Her anger is terrible. No one in the Seven Worlds can rage as she does."

What will she have? wondered Alec. He decided to take no chances.

"Orange Blossom," he whispered. "Get me a cord and a knife and bring them to my bed."

She drew in her breath. "My lord must not end his life."

"Don't be daft. I mean, That is not my will. Do my bidding if you wish to help me."

The girl brought what he wanted so discreetly

that he was able in a matter of seconds to bore a second hole in the can, thread the cord, hang it round his neck and tuck the can into his pyjama jacket. It looked weird, but at least it was safe. He could see and feel it all the time. Now for the night.

He did not have to wait long. In the middle of the feasting, the dancing, singing and music came to an abrupt halt as Maimunah strode in and confronted Alec. She was stern – yet laughing. Alec was bewildered.

"The time has come, O Al Ek. We shall be wed. We shall share our possessions, our treasures – my palace is yours. Your . . ."

Alec broke in, suspecting what this was leading to. "But my . . ." he gulped, "my wife . . ."

Maimunah grinned wickedly: "She is far away . . ."

Alec's brain spun.

"But I swore on oath to her to look at no other."

"Then divorce her."

"But she will demand her dowry money back."

"I will give you treasure enough to divorce a score of wives. Do not deny me!" she coaxed.

She turned and called.

"Ali."

An enormous slave, sword drawn, stepped forward. Alec felt the cold chill spread through his stomach.

"Call the Kadi. We shall have divorce and marriage in one. And," she turned the full blaze of her eyes on Alec, "after that . . ."

There was a moment's awful silence, then the

crowd at the entrance arch began to part to make way for a procession of men in sombre robes and large turbans. One in front, tall and imposing, walked with a great book in front of him, his face bent down towards its pages.

As he reached the centre of the chamber, he suddenly looked up. Alec blinked. Here was no ancient bearded face, but instead lean-jawed olive-green handsome features dominated by powerful black slanting eyebrows.

Maimunah screamed.

"Jujuru! Son of a Thousand Pigs!"

He laughed, and the sound reverberated through the palace.

"O Daughter of Calamity. It is indeed. I am here to rescue this youth, this Son of Worthy Parents, from your claws."

"Ali!" yelled Maimunah. And a score of male slaves sprang into a circle round them, scimitars flashing in the lamp light.

In that instant, Jujuru threw off his kadi's robes. His followers did the same. Like him, they were dressed in emerald green armour and drew long, pointed swords which they whirled round their heads with a shattering cry of "In the name of Dahnash, King of the Universe."

From beneath his bed Alec watched the battle through half-closed eyes. Maimunah launched herself at Jujuru with all the enthusiasm of someone greeting an old friend, or foe.

Two of his warriors leapt in her path, swords

thrusting. But with a sweep of her arm she threw them to left and right. As they landed, they burst into flames and shrivelled down to a pile of cinders. Alec closed his eyes.

The din of clashing swords was overlaid with tremendous explosions; balls of fire spun through the air as Maimunah and Jujuru got into their stride. With a crash, the roof fell in. Alec thanked his lucky stars he was under the bed. Walls disintegrated, curtains blazed into flames. The whole palace was falling apart. And still neither side would yield. The death toll was appalling and yet the number of fighters never seemed to diminish.

Gritting his teeth, Alec grasped the front legs of the bed and began to steer it towards a great gap in one wall where the starlit night showed through.

He had just reached it when he heard a great cry of rage from both sides.

Now was no time for hesitation or fear. He scrambled up, threw himself on the bed, pulled out the can on its cord and uttered the old magic words:

"Salaam Aleikum, O Abu Salem."

With a jerk the bed was airborne, soaring into the velvet darkness. Behind him smoke and flames poured from the oasis. In the east he saw the grey of dawn. He headed towards it, urging the bed onwards.

With first light he stared at his watch, shook it and looked at it again. It was exactly five past ten.

Chapter Six

Five past ten? Alec shook his watch again and held it to his ear. It was going.

Then he looked down from the bed, heading east at a fair cruising speed. Dawn was coming up under the curtain of night, pearl grey, mauve, pink, red where the first rays of the sun began to show. So why was it five past ten? Someone was playing tricks with time. What did it mean?

Then he forgot all about the time as he saw a broad swathe of green across the dark brown of the sands below. Palm trees nodded in the faint breeze, green fields, orchards. There was the sparkle of deep running water. This must be the Nile. Yes, there in the morning haze, feet planted in waves of sand, were the Pyramids, and that must be the Sphinx, huge head just showing.

Then he was over the great river and on to the east again; long narrow lagoons, reddish-brown hills. His mind went back to his watch.

He'd taken off at ten o'clock. That was three days ago. He'd spent three nights in the Palace of Delights, he was sure. And yet his watch had moved only five minutes – unless dawn came up at

10 a.m. in Egypt. No, he didn't believe that. Time must be moving at two speeds, one on his watch, the other in real life. *Real life?*

The hills fell behind and he was over the sea, stretching away silvery-blue to north and south. This must be the Red Sea. But that was crazy. When he'd started, he'd seen jet planes. He'd been buzzed, and worse, by US aircraft over the Med. But down there on the water were no tankers, no big ships, just dhows with their sails hanging limp in the morning air, the helmsman leaning on the tiller.

Beyond the water, more sand, dune after dune like waves, and, small as specks moving over the ridges, were strings of camels. Time wasn't only moving at two speeds, it was going backwards to an older, quieter, more peaceful time.

As he came in low over the desert, the heat began to strike upwards. The bed began to rise and fall on thermals. Then his heart stopped as a blood-curdling series of yells came from beneath him.

Over the next ridge, Alec looked down in alarm to see someone in a white robe like a long shirt, flapping as he tried frantically to scramble up the slope in the loose sand.

Behind him, whooping and laughing, came a group of horsemen, wild horses straining and foaming at the mouth, wild riders, cracking whips, waving drawn swords.

Their quarry stumbled, halted and fell to the ground exhausted and the hunters closed in, riding a tight circle around him, bending low to sweep with their blades inches from his body while he screamed in fear.

Something horrible was going to happen. Someone about as old as himself was about to get skewered and sliced to ribbons. Alec felt sick. He closed his eyes. All he wanted to do was zoom away.

At that moment, the can hanging round his neck came to life, crackling and spilling out words.

"Alec, O Alec, save!"

Despite himself, despite his nausea and terror, Alec brought the bed round in a tight circle, pointed it downwards to the desert and came in out of the dawn sunlight. He had a brief vision of the boy's face glaring upwards, eyes wide in fear and amazement.

Then, thump, thump, the bed rocked as the foot slammed into the first horseman, and the second. From below came howls of anguish. But now Alec laughed and swung the bed round again. He had it under perfect control and he was going to destroy the bandits below, utterly.

In he came, but they were not waiting for him. He saw only their broad backs bent over the horses' heads as they flogged them up the dune slope and away to vanish in the sand folds beyond.

He brought the bed down to a perfect four-point landing. Two crumpled shapes lay on the sand, the horses restlessly shifting to and fro nearby. Alec did not look too closely.

Instead his eye caught the boy he had just saved,

crouched on the ground before him, his back arched in submission.

"O Brave and Most Generous of Men. Blessed be the mother who bore thee, O Saviour, O Mighty One."

Alec was totally embarrassed.

"Rise," he commanded.

The boy's head came up suddenly at the sound of his voice. He stared, Alec stared. The boy began again:

"Blessed be . . ."

Then he stopped, leapt to his feet, grabbed Alec by the shoulders.

"Alec! It's you! I knew you'd come."

Chapter Seven

"Don't you remember me?"

Alec did. It all came back in a rush, a mixture of pleasure, irritation, confusion, embarrassment at past events.

It was Abu Salem's tearaway son.

"Abdul!" he yelled in surprise. "What are you doing here, Abdul? Who are these blokes? Why were they trying to kebab you?"

Abdul shook his head at the thought. "Alec, they belong to El Jawan's band. He's the biggest, fiercest robber chief between Cairo, Damascus and Baghdad. There are forty of his men and they are awesome. If the Caliph could lay hands on them, they'd be impaled on the spot."

"But why? You've got nothing they could steal."

"Ha, just using me for practice, Alec."

"Anyway," Alec took charge. "Look, get on the bed and let's get out of here."

Still bewildered, Abdul joined Alec on the bed. But for once, the bed refused to move. It would not stir. It remained fast on the sand. Abdul looked at Alec.

"Come on, let's move, Alec." Then he laughed. "Someone's put a spell on it, Alec."

Alec, highly irritated, nodded. "Yeah, but who?"

"Could be one of any number of people. No time to stop and puzzle that out, Alec. Come on."

He slipped off the bed, marched over to the robbers' horses, which now stood motionless by their masters' bodies. Quickly, skilfully, he lashed the two animals together. Then he came back to the bed.

"OK. Now lift. Right?"

Together they stowed the bed on the horses' backs. Abdul took the reins of the left-hand mount.

"Come on, let's get away."

They climbed the ridge and, from its summit, surveyed the desert before them. It stretched away, in rolling emptiness to the horizon, dim with heat haze. Now they began the descent. Abdul pointed ahead, to a narrow track, white among the sand.

"There, for a start."

As they began to pick their way down the track, Abdul turned again to Alec.

"You've come to help Father, haven't you, Alec? I guessed you wouldn't let him down. Believe me, he's in deep, deep trouble."

"I know," said Alec, "but what has he done?"

"I don't know. Nobody tells me anything."

"But where is he?"

Abdul looked ashamed, then said:

"Banged up in an old copper bottle at the bottom of the Secret Sea off the Coast of Mahgrib."

"And where's Mahgrib?"

"Over there," Abdul laughed and pointed west. "Two or three thousand miles."

"Oh no," answered Alec, "we'll never make it. There isn't time."

"What d'you mean? There isn't time?"

Alec looked at Abdul in despair. "All I know is I've got an hour to save him in. I don't know why. But that's what I have."

"An hour?" asked Abdul.

"That's it. Now this is the crazy bit. I reckon I've been here over three days. But my watch has only moved three minutes since I left home. And it hasn't stopped. I don't understand it."

"Ah," Abdul nodded as if all was crystal clear. "Ins time, that's human time, and djinn time, that's spirit time, are different. One hour human time equals one thousand hours spirit time." He thought a moment. "If that's right and you're here for one hour human time, then we have, let's see, forty days djinn time, and that means forty nights as well."

He jerked on the reins. "We might just do it unless these nags give up on us. But first, Alec, we have to get over the Red Sea."

Alec stared at Abdul. Abu's son, as he knew from the past, was a very dodgy sort of character. But right now Abdul was all he had.

"Haven't you any idea why Abu Salem's in prison?"

Abdul shrugged. "Something to do with the Everlasting Conflict."

60

Alec's mouth fell open: "The which?"

"You know, Good versus Evil, Right versus Wrong. Being going on since the Dawn of Time. First it was Eiblis against the Most High, then Rajmus and the King of the Sea versus Suleiman the Son of David. Now it's Dahnash and Ibn Jann. Don't ask me to explain who's what. I keep out of politics."

"But, Abdul, you've got to be on one side or the other . . ."

Abdul laughed scornfully. "Evil schemeevil, they both reckon they're in the right. And I tell you, they both order you about something rotten. Anyway, Alec, you're OK. You've come over to help out the old man, so you're all right in my book."

He pointed west.

"Let's go. We've enough food and water on these nags to keep us going till we find an oasis. Something's bound to turn up."

And it did.

Suddenly over the ridge to their left and right rose lines of horsemen. Yelling and howling, the riders came pouring down to surround them.

Alec grabbed the horses' reins.

"Let's get out of here, Abdul."

Abdul shook his head. "Forget it. That's El Jawan himself. We've had it."

The leader of the robber band swung off his horse and planted himself, legs astride, in front of them. Alec gazed up at him in awe. El Jawan was six foot six at least, and ugly as sin, with whiskers like the bristles on a wild hog. He was a man of few words. Pointing to Alec, he said:

"Dog and son of a dog. You destroyed two of my noblest warriors."

Alec's voice dwindled to a squeak.

"I'm sorry, sir. I mean, this humble slave throws himself on your infinite mercy, Most Chivalrous of Lords. It was an Act of God."

"Oh, blasphemy," shouted the men behind El Jawan. "He swooped down from the sky and smote them."

El Jawan looked thoughtful for a moment.

"Are you ins or djinn, man or spirit?" he demanded.

"I may not say," quavered Alec.

A sudden smile split the evil face into two.

"We shall find out then. If you are human you shall die. But out of our magnanimity you shall have a choice of death."

He beckoned to one of the band, who rushed forward, with pen and paper.

"Now write down: 'Two thousand lashes till the skin melts and the bones start forth; beheading; impaling upon a stake; roasting over a slow fire; boiling in oil'."

The paper was torn into small pieces and placed inside a turban and this was held out to Alec.

"Choose," said El Jawan.

"I would rather not, O Worthiest of . . ."

"*Choose!*" roared the robber chief.

Idiotically Alec plunged his hand into the greasy interior of the turban and came out with a folded scrap of paper. El Jawan tore it from his fingers and read out:

"Boiling in oil."

He turned to his followers. "Light the fire. Get the cauldron filled. Waste no time. I am agog to discover the nature of this worm."

"O Most Excellent of Brigands," said one of the band. "There is no oil left. We are waiting for the next caravan to help ourselves to fresh supplies."

El Jawan held out the turban again.

"Choose again."

Alec shook his head.

"It is unlucky to choose twice. The choice once made must be accepted. I prefer to be boiled in oil."

One of the robbers spoke humbly:

"O Mighty One. He is right. It must be oil or nothing."

El Jawan's face creased in rage and frustration.

"Make camp. We await the caravan."

"But Lord of Mercy," Alec spoke quickly. "That is not needful. I can tell you how to find oil."

"Hey, shut up, you crazy man," whispered Abdul.

"Shut up yourself," Alec whispered back.

Turning to El Jawan, he raised both arms. Then he pointed down to the sands.

"Beneath this desert lies more oil than you have ever dreamt of, O El Jawan. Only let your followers dig, and dig, and before you have time to think, oil will gush forth from the centre of the earth. Instead of living your lives in danger and toil and strife, the treasure you will find will keep your men like sultans for as long as you remain on this world."

For a moment El Jawan stared suspiciously at Alec, then he appeared to reflect a moment. Then he decided. Turning to his men, he said:

"Dig!"

Such was his command over these hairy men that, within minutes, the surface of the sand between the dunes was flung aside to a depth of several feet. Every member of the band leapt into the excavation, digging with swords, knife blades, trowels, spades, which appeared like magic from their saddle bags.

"Look at that." Abdul spoke in awe as he and Alec retreated with their pack horses from the side of the growing trench. As the forty thieves struggled to dig deeper, so Alec and Abdul drew back up the slope, which threatened to slide down into the mighty hole.

"A miracle," came a shout from beneath them.

In the depths of the dig, the sand had suddenly darkened and become moist and mud like. With yells and roars of excitement, the robbers dug like maniacs. Now the bed of the trench was awash in thick black liquid.

Suddenly, from far down, there was a muttering and rumbling.

"Come on, Abdul." Alec had a sudden premonition of what was to come. "Let's get out of here."

Dragging at the reins he scrambled up past the

madly digging outlaws towards the crest of the ridge.

"Hang about, man!" retorted Abdul. Springing to one side, he cut the tethering ropes of two of the finest mounts.

"Get on board," he told Alec.

"I can't ride," protested Alec.

"So boil then!"

Abdul kicked his heels into the horse's side. It lunged forward dragging packhorses and bed over the ridge. Alec had no choice. Shoving a foot into the stirrup, he wildly swung his leg over the broad back of the second horse, which was already scrabbling up the slope.

Once mounted, he clung on like grim death as they slithered and bounded down the other side. With a clatter of loose stones, they were down in the valley beyond and away at a smart trot. A hundred yards further on, Abdul reined in and waved for Alec to look back. Behind them over the top of the ridge, hundreds of feet into the air, rose a mighty black column of gushing oil.

Abdul began to laugh.

"You are magic, Alec!"

That night, the next night and the next they camped under the stars and the awesome canopy of velvet darkness. They lived off dried dates and small mouthfuls of water from the skins tied to their saddles. Moving on while it was still dark, resting in the shelter of rocks in the heat of noon, they moved west.

And early on the fourth day, a flash of light shone in front of them below two jagged brown hills. It was the rising sun on water.

Alec urged his horse forward.

"Abdul, come on. It's the sea, the sea."

But just as they came within a score of yards from the hills, and the blue waters of the sea were clearly visible beyond them, Abdul suddenly turned, and jerking on the reins of the packhorses took off in a wide circle away to the south. Bouncing and swaying on their backs went Alec's precious magic bed.

"Abdul," shouted Alec. "Where are you going, you idiot?"

Abdul, riding hard, simply shouted back over his shoulder.

"Run for your life, Alec!"

Alec, bewildered, began to rein in his horse. But before he could turn, he was plucked from his saddle and jerked, a hundred feet into the air, by a force which crushed him at the waist like a giant hand.

It *was* a giant hand. One of the hills had come to life and grown a monstrous face with cavernous mouth, enormous squashed nose and red glaring eyes. It was towards these eyes and the gaping mouth with its ghastly jagged teeth that he was being carried.

"Let me go," he screamed.

And in the next second, it did.

Chapter Eight

Alec fell, and fell, turning over and over screeching and laughing hysterically in his fear. As he whirled round and round he caught glimpses of the rocky foot of the hill, which flew towards him as if reaching out to tear and smash him to bits.

He felt a terrific shock, and thought: "This is it. I've had it. Now I know what it's like being dead." But it wasn't and he wasn't. Instead he hung in mid-air, caught as if by some gigantic grab. His eyes searched wildly round and his thoughts stopped. Around his middle curled two grotesque, brown, sausage-like shapes. They could only be – yes, they had to be – fingers. He could see the nails, and the dirt under them.

Before he could upset himself, he was raised up again rushing through the air to halt just feet away from those glowing red eyes and the cave-like mouth. There came a gale of foul breath, the jagged teeth showed themselves. Then a voice spoke:

"O child of guile and iniquity. You thought to escape by that ancient trick. Let me go! Ho ho. And I nearly did."

"Oh no," gasped Alec, feeling his stomach pinched

into his backbone. "O Emir of Mercy, the warmth of your welcome disordered my wits. I throw myself on your mercy."

"That is well spoken," rumbled the voice. He was held closer to the eyes. The red veins stood out like rivers in the whites.

"Are you ins or djinn, human or spirit?"

This time, Alec was prepared.

"O Estimable Father, I am one of the Children of Adam, a traveller."

"What is thy name?"

"The slave who dares address you is called Alec Bowden."

"Hallek BaHdeen?"

The great brown mass shook with laughter. What was the joke about his name, he wondered. Then that thought was driven from his mind by another. I'm going to fall again!

His trembling was observed. The voice suddenly became quieter.

"What ails you, Son? Are you not well? Sit down."

Sit down?

"I will clear you a space." Another hand appeared, thrusting past Alec to reach out to the hill which stood some twenty feet away. With a single sweep, the summit was swept away in a cloud of rock and sand. In its place was a flat area about ten yards square. And on to this, Alec felt himself set down.

He lay panting, till the pain in his guts began to

ease. Across the gap, the red eyes regarded him for a second, then the mountainous body quivered with laughter again.

"May I be forgiven. It is impolite to mock a traveller and his name."

"What's wrong with my name?" demanded Alec.

"In our tongue, it signifies one who comes late."

Alec started to laugh himself now. It was funny, even if it was true.

"What is thy name, O Compassionate One?" he asked.

"I am called El Samit, the Silent One. For I cannot abide those who talk too much. I never speak more than is necessary. You, O Al Ek, are a Fortunate Traveller. If I were a ghoul I might have eaten you alive. Ghouls love human flesh – even better after being buried a while. But I am a ghoul-marid. My mother was a ghoul, my father a giant. A strange marriage it is said, but a respectable and happy one. Which is why I am good-tempered, and as much cannot be said about ghouls and marids in general. What is more, they talk too much, whereas I tend to be quiet and reflective, even taciturn, as you have have noticed."

Before Alec could agree, the ghoul-marid went on. "Anyway, I do not like raw meat. I prefer mine cooked. And since you are not cooked, there's an end to it. In addition, you are, given the chance, very polite, which is more than I can say for a good many of the Children of Adam, a rude bunch who never stop chattering."

El Samit sighed, causing a small hurricane which almost swept Alec from his ledge, then continued.

"Remember that, O Son of Worthy Parents. Magic is important in this world, but politeness is the greatest gift. Wherever you do, among men or spirits, ins or djinn, always be polite."

Alec suddenly got a word in

"I read of djinns, afrits, ghouls and marids in the Arabian Nights, the Thousand and One . . ."

"What?" roared El Samit, his vast nose curling in contempt. "That book of Shame? All those immoral women, making monkeys of their good husbands, and the bad language, the gluttony, the wickedness. Oh women, women. That is why I never married."

"But Worthy Father," protested Alec, "it is only a story."

"Only? *Only?* How little do you know of stories and the harm they can do! But who can resist them? You, O Al Ek, must tell me yours. I have stood here for twenty years and hardly heard a single story. Tell me yours. What are you doing here in this place and age?"

"It is a long story."

"All the better. Tell on."

So Alec told, and told until his head began to spin. It was now some time since he had eaten. But El Samit listened with such attention that he felt compelled to go on.

When he came to his days in the Palace of Delight, the ghoul-marid burst out.

"Ah, Maimunah, Maimunah. Who has not heard

70

tell of her? You were lucky to have escaped in one piece. But, tell me, why have you come here?"

Alec told of his search for Abu Salem. "You may not have heard of him," he said politely.

"What?" rumbled El Samit, "but for sure I know Abu Salem. I know everyone in our realm." He went on in a slightly hushed voice as if remembering. "I played polo for Djinnistan for two centuries. I met everyone. Not now though," he added with regret.

"Will my Worthy Uncle be good enough to tell me why?" asked Alec.

"Headaches," said the ghoul-marid tersely. "From the ball," he added by way of explanation.

"But I thought you used a mallet for polo," said Alec, perplexed.

"Mallets," snorted El Samit, "are for cowards, Ah, those days, to take a pass from the wing and head it clean into the net and hear the crowd roar, while my fellow players embraced me. Still those were good times. But no more."

He nodded.

"Abu Salem is a worthy man. Unlike his son Abdul, a limb of Shaitan, whom I saw running away with your horses and baggage, including that remarkable bed."

"He was afraid," explained Alec unwillingly.

"With good reason. Bad conscience. Like a lot of the young djinns these days, he runs with the hare and hunts with the hounds."

"You mean he works for both sides."

"Indeed, or rather belongs to neither side but blows with the wind." El Samit brooded for a while, then asked: "Where did you say Abu Salem was imprisoned?"

"In a copper jar under the Secret Sea off the coast of Mahgrib," replied Alec.

"Alas, O Al Ek, Mahgrib is beyond my range. But I can take you to Damascus."

"Why should I go to Damascus?" asked Alec, puzzled.

"For a good reason. It is there that your precious bed has been taken, no doubt to end up in the Thieves' Market and be sold to the highest bidder."

"But how can I get it back?" demanded Alec, alarmed. "I wouldn't be able to find the market even, let alone my bed."

"In Damascus," went on El Samit, "you will also find Abdul Salem, your so-called servant and friend. He will know where your bed has gone."

The ghoul-marid's eyes closed as if the effort of thinking wearied him. Alec looked at his watch. It was now ten past ten. His precious hour was draining away. Then he realized El Samit was watching him.

"Why do you look so often at that bracelet?"

"It tells me how time is passing."

"Then throw it away, O Worthy Youth. Time is an enemy. If it is your destiny to rescue Abu Salem, you will do it within the appointed span. If it is not your destiny, then a thousand years will not be enough.

"What I can tell you is that your destiny points to Damascus, and to Damascus I will gladly take you.

"But first," rumbled El Samit, "we must eat."

He chortled at the dismay on Alec's face and reassured him. "No grave robbings, O Honoured Guest. Just a simple meal, an appetising morsel, chicken stuffed with rice, butter and almonds, fried fish in bread, spiced mincemeat cakes, fillet of mutton in tomato rice, then sugar tart, biscuit, pomegranate pulp, sherbert scented with rose water, date jam, bananas, figs, dates and grapes . . ."

It was tasty, and it was exciting, since every ten seconds El Samit's massive hairy arm would shoot across the gap and scoop up several dishes and empty them down the great gulf of his mouth.

Still, Alec did well and, as his hunger vanished, his confidence returned. So far he had met enemies and dodgy characters. No one was what they seemed. But he had met the most unlikely friends.

"To aid digestion," said the ghoul-marid, "let us tell riddles. You may begin."

Alec racked his brains. He always had this trouble at school – couldn't think of a single riddle, then remembered dozens at three o'clock the next morning.

Slowly he began to remember. But it wasn't so simple. Riddles about umbrellas, kettles, escalators and number ten buses just caused El Samit's eyes to glaze over. Even Humphrey, the camel with three humps, left him cold.

El Samit was equally frustrated when Alec didn't know how many verses there were in each book of the Koran. He shook his head and muttered about ignorant young people.

But in the end they struck common ground.
How deep is the ocean? asked El Samit (a stone's throw).
What can run but not walk? asked Alec (a river).
What dies when it breathes fresh air? (a fish).
What has teeth but no mouth? (a comb).

The riddling lasted into the afternoon till Alec fell asleep in the shade of El Samit's great hand, to wake when the sun was setting.

"Now, O Youth of Virtuous Parents, your quest begins again. Fear not, for I will tell you something of value. Your name is not only Al Ek Bahdeen, One Who Comes Late. It may also be spoken thus, El Akbar Din, which signifies One of Great Faith.

"If you are set on rescuing Abu Salem your slave . . ."

"I am," said Alec.

"Then there will be dangers."

El Samit plucked a large hair tuft from his bristly chin and held it out. Alec took it, mystified.

"Keep that with care. There may be a time when you need help desperately. Burn these hairs and I will come to your aid."

Alec tucked the hair tuft into his pyjama pocket.

"Thank you, O Venerable One. And now, let us go to Damascus."

Chapter Nine

Damascus shone white, blue and gold in the early sunlight as El Samit, with Alec tucked stiflingly into one of his smelly pockets, landed on the broad meadow in front of the city.

The ghoul-marid extracted Alec, brushed him down and set him on the grass, then, pointing to the city gates, he said:

"In the back streets of this City of Sin you will find Abdul Salem, and soon. And I will give you some advice on what to do.

"First go boldly and look neither to left nor right. When you see a quick movement in the corner of your left eye, turn quickly. He will be there. When you find him you must then do this."

The ghoul-marid bent close to Alec and whispered slowly in his ear. Then he straightened up, pausing a moment to ruffle his hair, almost tipping him over, and said:

"May joy abide with you and the Invisible Strength protect you – O Akbar Din."

Then, with an explosion like an ancient locomotive letting off steam, he was gone.

Taking a deep breath, Alec joined the great

throng of market people with their donkeys and camels, all piled high with baskets and bundles. The traders greeted one another raucously and barracked the guards with a stream of amiable insults as they shoved through the city gates. No one seemed to notice Alec, and the sheer weight of the crowd carried him through the narrow streets. They reached a large square.

Here the pressure eased as groups of people set off in different directions, heading for the various markets.

Dodging for a moment out of the stream of hurrying folk, Alec found a quiet corner and made a swift check. Can? OK, still hanging by the gold cord Orange Blossom had given him in the Palace of Delights.

Now, watch? Still on his wrist and showing twelve minutes past ten. While the wheel of days moved slowly, the small circle of human clock time sneaked round at its own speed.

But he had to forget the time and push on. He set out across the square, looking always straight in front of him, as El Samit had told him.

He had nearly reached the farther side when a quick movement to his left made him swing round. There, lurking in the shade of a potter's shop was none other than Abdul Salem. The shock of seeing him drove El Samit's advice from his mind for a second.

"Abdul! Abdul!" he called. "I want a word with you."

But at the sound of Alec's voice, Abdul turned and ran like a hare into the narrow alley by the shop.

Now Alec recalled what El Samit had whispered in his ear. Opening his mouth wide, he yelled:

"Help me, good people. A robber has stolen all I have. The boy running in the alley by the potters. Catch him. Catch him."

In the narrow lane, the crowd surged like a tide waving and shouting. But after only a few seconds, out of the confusion came the bedraggled figure of Abdul, clothes torn and one eye half closed. He was held firmly by two huge men with curved scimitars in their belts and followed by a mass of buyers and sellers.

"Who has been robbed?" demanded one of the guards.

"I have," called Alec.

"Is this the thief?"

"It is," Alec forced out the words, trying not to look at Abdul's face which was now white and running with sweat.

"Then he shall lose one hand or two, according to what he has stolen."

Now Alec turned white.

"No," he gasped.

The guard looked at him astonished. "It is the Law, O Youth."

"No, I don't want that," Alec forced the words out. Amid the silence that followed an old man spoke.

"Allah is just. We are taught that a thief may be pardoned."

The guard looked down at Alec.

"Do you pardon him?"

"If he comes with me and confesses all," he said slowly, looking now at Abdul's face which had got back its colour.

A look of disappointment crossed the guard's face. "Mercy is Blessed," he said. Abdul, released, threw himself down at Alec's feet and the crowd, shaking heads and chattering, gradually moved away.

"Get up, you clown," hissed Alec.

"If my master permits," muttered Abdul and unfolded himself, eyeing Alec with new respect.

"You come with me," Alec grabbed Abdul's arm, hauled him up and dragged him away from the square. In a side street he gathered a handful of Abdul's tunic in one hand and pulled him to and fro.

"Now you are going to tell the truth, or I call the boys with the blades back. They'll take off your arm and hit you with the wet end."

Abdul spoke humbly. "Truth is golden."

"Where's my bed? Why did you sell it? How are we going to save your dad while you are clowning round the Middle East?"

"The bed was stolen from me." He jerked his thumb vaguely to the south.

"What, El Jawan again?"

"Uh-uh. A new bunch, all masked. Could have been girls."

"Pull the other."

"You don't know this part of the world, Alec."

"So, everything's gone, bed and all?"

"Well," said Abdul, "I sort of know where the bed is."

"Tell me.

"Been sold to the Wali."

"The which?"

"Chief of Police. He always gets first pick of what's new in the Thieves' Market. His men carried it off to his house."

"Right," Alec was masterful. "You are going in there, right now, and you are going to get that bed back, by fair means or foul."

To his astonishment, Abdul grinned slyly, then shook his head.

"Correction. You, not me. You are the only one who can move that bed. You have to go in there."

Alec looked up at the sky, speechless, then down at his pyjamas.

"I'd be spotted."

"Uh-uh. You go in in disguise."

"Disguise?"

"Yeah. Trust me." Abdul's spirits had magically recovered. Once again he was in charge. He raised a hand.

"Come with me."

Ten minutes of turning, twisting, ducking, diving, pushing and shoving, being cursed and cursing back, brought them to a square on the far side of the city.

"Wait here, Alec," muttered Abdul, "while I get your outfit."

Before Alec could demand more details, he had vanished.

Left alone, Alec looked about him. This square was quieter than the others. It had small plots of grass and flowers. No crowds here, just groups of richly dressed men, gravely talking and listening. This must be the jewellers' market, or the goldsmiths', or stockbrokers' maybe. Did they have stockbrokers in the Middle Ages?

Alec's theories were suddenly shattered when a man, escorted by armed soldiers, led a string of young people out into the market. They were black, or white, or brown, the males stripped to the waist, the females gracefully veiled and wearing bangles, many with gold and silver from wrist to elbow.

There was a hush as he began to speak, turning and beckoning. One by one the young people stepped forward, marched up and down, turned round, faced this way and that.

But it was when one of the fat merchants stepped forward and squeezed a girl's bottom reflectively that light dawned on Alec.

"Why, it's the slave market."

"In one," Abdul spoke just behind him. He had a bundle under his arm. "Any minute now the Wali himself'll be here to do a bit of buying. We play our cards right, we'll be in."

Alec seized Abdul by the neck.

"You are going to sell me to the Wali?"

"Right. Listen, get rid of your twentieth-century

fantasies. There is nothing dishonourable in slavery. I'm a slave. So's Dad. Slaves get treated well. At least some do. Most of the time. Some get freed – in time. Some get rich."

Alec saw the smile that came and went with the outrageous words. He decided to play it straight. "Listen, you crook. I'm free. I intend to stay that way.

"Right on. This is just a device. You stay there just as long as it takes you to get to that bed and fly out. OK? Now, put these things on and I'll lead you in to the market. Hey, look who's there, the Wali himself."

"What?" jeered Alec, "that dirty old man? He's gross."

"You don't even have to like him. Just deceive him."

"But suppose he buys someone else? The competition's pretty," Alec hesitated, "hot."

"No chance. He's so mean. The Wali goes for rock bottom prices. He'a a byword. It'll be a doddle. Now get down behind this wall here and get changed. These can go on over your pyjamas."

Crouched by the wall, Alec stared aghast as Abdul held out, one by one, a chemise, baggy flimsy pantaloons, a head-dress and, lastly, a veil.

"But these are girl's clothes," he squeaked.

Abdul stared at him as if baffled.

"Don't you understand, man? The bed is in the harem."

"The *harem*?" Alec's voice had almost vanished.

"Hey, keep it like that, Alec, that pitch is just right."

"The harem," Alec said again, his voice sliding down the scale. "No way."

Abdul jabbed a finger in Alec's chest.

"Tell me, do you really want to help my father, your genie, your old pal, or is this friendship talk just a load of rubbish?"

"You know I do. But do I have to put this girls' stuff on?"

"Alec, do I have to draw you a diagram? The bed's in the harem, right?"

"Right."

"There are two ways you get into a harem. One is dressed as a girl. The other is as a boy, but sort of modified. Get it?"

Alec's mouth fell open, then closed with a click.

"Give me the clothes," he said.

Chapter Ten

"Behold this milk-white pearl, O Lords of Noble Ancestry." Abdul pulled Alec into the centre of the square, calling out as he moved forward. "Brought from the West, a Christian maid," Abdul licked his lips.

The circle of men looked at Alec. Their eyes were shrewd, curious. Some looked kindly, some eyes had a lewd glint, some were hard as stone. Was he glad about the veil. His cheeks burned, not least at Abdul's language.

"Behold the pale skin with peach down on it, the eyes, delicate grey as the dawn."

He broke off and muttered to Alec.

"Turn round, wiggle your hips, shake it about. You are supposed to be a girl."

Alec did as instructed. One man raised his eyebrows as if puzzled, another looked away. Most just stared impassively. But one stepped forward, fingers twitching.

"Emir. It is not permitted to touch," Abdul stepped smartly in front of Alec. "Such is the value of this slave, whose name is Daybreak . . ."

Daybreak? Alec cringed inwardly.

". . . that I have made her two promises. First, that she shall not be handled. Second, that she herself shall choose he who shall buy her."

"How much?"

Alec could not be sure but the voice seemed to come from the depths of the Wali's thick, white beard.

"Five hundred dinars, my masters. I say that in sorrow for I have already paid out of my own purse a thousand gold coins for her nourishment and education. See her garments, the Kashmir belt, the Kufa silks, the veil from Mosul, the opals, sapphires at her throat . . ."

"Hah," sneered a fat man with an evil smile, "I'll give you three hundred and that is twice her worth. Look at her arms – thin as twigs, camel-backed, flat-chested, no buttocks to speak of . . . which hospital did you find her in?"

Alec, cut to the quick, burst out.

"Fear not, O Gross One, I am not for thee. Hath not the poet said:

"Slave I may be, but 'tis hard,
To yield one's beauty to a tub of lard."

The square rocked with laughter. The fat man, fuming, walked away. Alec pressed home with:

"I will be sold to none other than the excellent El Khalid, Wali of this City, a man known throughout the Seven Kingdoms for his kindness, his generosity, his nobility and respect for justice."

A younger man stepped forward.

"This slave has a witty tongue. I have never heard a better, more entertaining description of our respected Wali. I will give you four hundred."

To Alec's amazement, Abdul seemed about to accept. Could he really be going to ruin the whole plan just for the sake of some extra ready cash? He decided to take no chances but spoke up again.

"I regret I must be sold to El Khalid and none other."

"Ha, then it's two hundred and not a dirhan more," rasped the Wali. He signalled to the tall slave who stood behind him and strode from the square.

Before Alec could gather his wits he was being led away in the same direction by the servant, while Abdul, money pocketed, had vanished. His escort tapped Alec on the shoulder and said good-humouredly:

"Stop wriggling your bum, Daybreak. Our respected Master isn't interested. You've been bought for the kitchen."

The next three days were pure hell for Alec. From dawn to nightfall when he was allowed to fall asleep on the kitchen floor, filthy clothes sticking to his body like a second skin, he worked. Or rather, he slaved. Now, he thought, I know what the word means.

Every job that was too menial for the other servants was given to him. His disguise was never penetrated because no one looked at him or talked to him. They called him, hit him, kicked him (it took a while to remember to answer to 'Daybreak'). But otherwise, they left him alone.

Hardest to bear, though, was none of these things. It was that he never left the kitchen or courtyard. The harem for which he had sacrificed so much, with its cool passages, and curtains, remained out of reach. There was no chance to sneak away and explore it.

But on the fourth day, when his watch showed nearly twenty past ten, he was ready for desperate measures. And that night his opportunity came.

The Wali was entertaining guests. All the food had been prepared. The other servants rushed to and fro. And the greasy dishes had not yet begun to pile up.

He had, he guessed, five minutes, djinn time, before his absence might be noticed or his presence required. He was wound up enough not to heed the risks.

He sneaked across the courtyard and through the doorway where he had seen the Wali's plump wives and plumper daughters come and go. In seconds he was in the harem and looking for the bedchambers.

He found the first with ease. And there in the middle of the floor, half screened by a curtain, was *his* bed. Racing across the room he leapt on to it, disregarding the black smears he made on the pillows.

"Get going," he ordered.

But the bed did not move. He spoke again, louder this time. But the bed stayed where it was.

Jumping from it he looked more closely and realised with a feeling of despair that it wasn't his bed. It was a copy.

He dived out of the bedroom and into the next. With the same results. In four separate chambers were four replicas of his bed. Where was the original?

From the kitchen he heard yells of "Daybreak!" Rushing back, he pretended to have come from the privy. He was lucky to get away with a blow that knocked him half across the fireplace.

That night he lay awake for an hour, grinding his teeth and thinking what he would do with the Wali, and with Abdul, in that order.

His wishes had some power. Next day, across the courtyard to the kitchen door, came a peddlar, an old crone in black.

She sold trinkets, exchanging lewd jokes with the female servants and eunuchs. Then she approached Alec.

"Well, my pretty one," she whispered. "Will you buy a bracelet for those lovely arms?"

Alec recoiled but his wrist was in an iron grip.

"Hey, Alec. What's happened with that bed? I've grown hair waiting."

Restraining himself, Alec told Abdul in a few choice whispered words what the hold-up was. Abdul swore quietly, then said:

"You'd better get out of here. Your cover won't last long."

"How, you clown?"

"Midnight. See that vine in the courtyard? Climb that. There'll be a ladder on the other side. I'll be there. We'll work something out."

The rest of the day dragged by. Alec made mistake after mistake, collected blow after blow, but didn't care. When dusk fell he was so weary he could barely keep his eyes open. Only an effort of will kept him awake and alert.

At last the kitchen, harem, the whole house, went quiet. One by one all the lights were snuffed out.

When the eunuch in charge of the kitchen was snoring across the door, Alec judged it was time.

From beyond the wall came a low whistle.

Alec took three quick steps across the kitchen, leapt over the sleeping eunuch, ran across the courtyard and scrambled up the vine like a monkey. Seconds later he was sliding down the ladder on the far side.

So hasty was he that he did not take in the warning shout from across the dark street.

He was seized round the middle, pulled violently off the ladder and flung so roughly across the saddle of a horse that the breath left his body.

Hooves clattered and the night was split by a yell of triumph.

"It is I, El Jawan. Now I take my revenge."

Chapter Eleven

Breathlessness, pain and total despair clamped Alec's mouth shut as the robber chief's horse carried him away across the city. From time to time El Jawan sang, snatches of song, martial, obscene, sentimental. Now and then he let out whoops of triumph.

"Like a peach from a tree while the watchman slept she fell into my hands. O Happy El Jawan. Revenge is sweet and the taste stays in the mouth."

How does he know it's me? The stupid thought kept running through Alec's mind as the city was left behind. El Jawan laughed at gates and guards and found his way easily through the great graveyard with its crumbling walls.

He sang again, louder this time, beating time on Alec's backside. Alec gritted his teeth and thought of different ways of destroying the robber chief, when he had the chance. Followed by the Wali and, last but not least, the son of Abu Salem.

A point of light ahead grew to a red circle. Then a camp fire gleamed through the palms of an oasis. Bursts of drunken song showed that the band was in bivouac and living it up.

As the chief rode in, a ragged cheer came from

the fire. El Jawan swung down from the saddle and hauled Alec down like a sack of kindling.

"A prize, a prize," crowed his followers. One stepped from the fire to examine Alec.

"A little dove – share and share alike, O Great One!"

"True, O Captain. Share and share alike," shouted the others.

Alec nearly passed out, then revived as El Jawan drew his scimitar and drove off the others.

"Look, but do not touch. This is not a prize but a hostage, a slave of that worm El Khalid. When he surrenders the magic bed which rightly belongs to me, as does its owner," he added in a breaking voice, "killer of two of the finest thieves in the Twenty One Kingdoms; when he gives up the bed and tells me where the owner is, he shall have his morsel back. Till then, do not touch."

Alec slept hardly at all until near dawn when the singing and shouting died down.

He had barely dozed for ten minutes when he was woken, fed meat and a crust, given a mouthful of water and put on to a mule. The mule was linked to El Jawan's charger by a long rope.

The chief mounted and told his followers:

"Hear me. I go with our hostage to Khorus. At noon, one of you ride to the city and deliver our terms to the Wali, in this letter. Give him three days."

"What if he says no?"

"Then it is share and share alike," grunted El Jawan, leering at the quivering Alec.

They rode all that day, camped in a small wood, ate more bread, meat, water, had a few hours sleep then went on again in the half light. At midday the domes and minarets of Khorus came into view above the dunes.

"Khorus, a famous place," laughed El Jawan. "Famous for hospitality and no questions asked of strangers. Its kings are chosen from the first stranger who comes after the death of the old one." He bellowed with laughter. "If I am lucky, I may arrive in time to be the chosen ruler."

Alec said nothing. His attention had been distracted.

Outside the great towered gates of the city a gigantic carpet had been spread in a wide meadow. Alec had never seen such a carpet before – at twenty pounds a square yard it would have cost a million.

Seated on the carpet appeared to be the whole population of the city, grouped around cauldrons and dishes, heaped with food of all kinds. Beyond the carpet was a dais with a throne surrounded by richly dressed courtiers.

And on the throne, a young king, scintillating in gold and jewels, a slender but magnificent figure.

"Oh Milk-White Day," growled El Jawan, "we come in time for the monthly feast. Everyone eats his fill without paying a penny."

He urged forward his horse, dragging Alec's mule behind it, and in minutes had tied both animals to a tree. Then he pulled Alec into an empty space on the carpet, near the throne. Alec needed no pulling.

He was famished. But not too famished to gape at his captor.

"Ho, rice cream," yodelled El Jawan. Seizing a big dish, he began to ladle the white mixture into his mouth, spattering moustache, beard and tunic liberally with it.

No accounting for taste, thought Alec, as he began to chew on a delicious chicken leg. He had never, ever seen so much rice pudding eaten so violently before.

Someone else was watching too. Suddenly a shadow fell across them. Alec looked up to see two armed guards glaring down.

"You two. Come."

"What's this? It is the King's feast," spluttered El Jawan. "All strangers are free to sit and eat in peace. What have we done to deserve this treatment?"

The guards reached down and hauled both to their feet.

"When the king frowns, run," joked one. "But just now, come."

The two of them were frog-marched through the guests, who scattered in confusion until they stood before the throne.

"Down."

The guards forced them flat on their faces. Alec heard a pleasant, yet masterful voice speak.

"Welcome to my court."

They struggled up. The king was very young but handsome; his face a delicate pink, his lips covered by a soft moustache. The eyes were sharp.

"Who are you?"

"The slave who dares address you, O King of Time, is called Maaruf, honest merchant of Mosul, and his niece Fatima for whom he has cared since her parents were taken by the Great Separator."

Liar, thought Alec.

"Liar," said the king. The multitude was now completely silent, all eating forgotten.

"No honest merchant ever wolfed his food, gulping delicacies like a hog and strewing it down his front," went on the stern voice, then, suddenly, the King shouted:

"I know you, El Jawan."

The crowd gasped.

"Vile robber whose crimes are infamous from Bassora to Aljirah. And this poor child is your prisoner. Or was. Now she is free."

From the crowd came a storm of applause.

"O Justice. Great is our King."

"Now, dog of a merchant, say farewell to your niece. And you, fairest of maidens, shall be taken to my harem and tended like a queen until I come to you. As for you, dog and son of dogs, the impaling stake awaits you."

Alec felt himself gently led away to the city gates, through the silent streets and under the ornamented arch of the palace entrance. In the dark of the harem he was surrounded by twittering girls' voices.

"What is thy name, O Princess?"

Alec gulped.

"Daybreak."

93

"Ah, a name of truth. You are fortunate, O Milk-White Face. We rejoice. Till now our king has taken no wives, neither has he honoured any of his slaves. Yet he is so fair. A thousand women would lay down their lives, and other things too for him. And now you are to be that one, O fortunate Daybreak."

Hands clapped. "Bring fresh robes, take Daybreak to the baths, wash her, dry her, powder her, scent her, make her ready for her Lord."

Paralysed by confusion and alarm, Alec was led through passage after passage till at last at the door of the baths he recovered his will and courage.

"It is my wish that I should prepare myself for the king alone."

"Oh no, that cannot be."

Alec stamped his foot.

"Shall I tell the king then that my first request was refused?"

There was a sudden silence.

"Leave my garments inside the door. Then close it and do not dare to look in."

Half an hour later, bathed and refreshed, the filth of the Wali's kitchen and the robber's lair removed, dressed a little unskilfully but adequately in the rich robes, Alec emerged into the passage.

Now the slaves had doubled in number, calling "Yu yu, such beauty". Under the veil, Alec blushed and hoped they had the decency to do the same.

Ahead there was music, laughter, singing. They came into a chamber smaller than the others, or perhaps it seemed smaller because of the size of the curtained bed.

On a low table were dishes, delicacies of every kind, flasks of wine and rosewater.

And seated behind the table, handsome in a loose robe, was the young king.

"Approach, fair one."

Alec's stomach turned to water. He could not move.

The King clapped his hands. The room emptied. The door closed. Now they were alone.

Uncoiling his long legs, the King came towards Alec and took his hands.

"At last, O precious one, we are alone."

Alec forced himself to speak.

"O King of Time. There is one problem."

"What is that, little one?"

"I am really a boy."

The king laughed.

"That is no problem."

I'm going to pass out, thought Alec.

"No problem at all," the king went on, "for I'm really a girl."

With a sweep the moustache was ripped off, the turban thrown aside, the long hair poured down and the green eyes flashed.

"Maimunah," gasped Alec.

Chapter Twelve

"O Prince of Excellence," she bowed low. "My days and nights have been long since last I saw you."

Alec looked at her. The handsome face was serious but the eyes had the old mocking glint. There was a lot he wanted to say, but right now he could not find words for it. He settled for:

"Blessed be the day of our meeting, O Maimunah."

"Your words are cold, Lord."

Alec's teeth began to grind. She must have read the expression in his eyes. She smiled roguishly.

"I would prolong this moment for a month of days, but," she nodded towards the heavily curtained bed, "O Al Ek, we must depart this place and upon the moment. Behind those curtains, with enough hashish up his nostrils to fell an elephant, is the true King of Khorus whose place and name I have borrowed.

"When he awakes, certain words will be said. We must be far from here. And besides, there is much to do."

"Too right," burst out Alec. "My bed, for example. Every time I get my hands on it, somebody whips it away . . ."

He stressed the word "somebody".

He raised his wrist and tapped his watch: "Let's fly to Damascus and get the bed back."

Maimunah shook her head.

"The bed is now – in Baghdad." She raised a slender, ringed hand. "Fear not, all is well. Tomorrow – or the next day, you will see it again."

As she spoke, Alec heard from behind the curtains a groan, then a sneeze. Maimunah smiled and held out her hand.

"It is time to go."

Alec shook his head.

"Not as a girl, O King."

Quickly he pulled off the chemise, the drawers, the veil, down to the familiar and reassuring blue and white pyjamas.

Maimunah took his hand and in that instant the walls, the palace, and the city beyond dissolved and fell away.

They were in the air and flying east. Behind them the sun was setting and giant shadows stretched across the sand, pointing their way.

Flying the bed was something. Flying like this with Maimunah was something else. There was no fear, no sense of height at all, only of space and freedom and the feeling that everything was possible. Below, the landscape whirled away, darkness fell and a great yellow moon rose, turning the sand to silver. They seemed to hover while the world turned.

He looked down. Soon the walls and towers of the fabulous city of Haroun El Rachid would appear, a place he knew so well from books; its palaces, its gilded river barges, crowded markets and cool gardens. Now he was going to see it as it was, when it was.

He felt special, important, powerful.

Then the sun came up, the dark raced away to the west. Alec looked down and saw, aghast, that they were over the sea. The djinniah had done it on him again.

"Maimunah," he gasped. She turned to him eyebrows raised.

"This isn't Baghdad, Maimunah, is it? We're over the Gulf. What's the game?"

"Game?" She smiled and squeezed his hand. "My lord is not pleased? I planned a diversion. A day, or two perhaps, in a small island palace, to recover from your – experiences."

Completely forgetting where he was, Alec tried to snatch his hand away, but she held him in a steely grip. "Fool," her voice was harsh. The old-world courtesy had gone. "Will you ruin everything? Come."

Alec felt a tremendous pull as she took them into a headlong dive.

"What's going on?" he yelled.

Maimunah said nothing, but then Alec saw, a score of feet away from them, a speeding figure, lean and green, purple cloak flying from its shoulders, heading straight at them.

"Maimunah, Daughter of Deceit. Release that young innocent you are about to corrupt."

98

"Ha, Jujuru, Father of Corruption yourself. Keep your foul hands far from this boy, who is under my protection."

While they shouted both wheeled and turned in the air like dog-fighting planes. Alec was swung this way and that, while earth, sea and sky spun round him.

"Machine-gun fire next," he thought idiotically.

Wrong. There was a mighty explosion, a ball of yellow smoke and flame just below them, lifting Maimunah and Alec a hundred feet into the air.

"Son of a thousand filthy pigs," snarled Maimunah. Lifting an arm, she sent a stream of thunderbolts which burst like anti-aircraft rockets round their attacker. Jujuru laughed insanely as he spun head over heels, then came at them again out of the sun.

He was firing with both fingers. The air round them sizzled and crackled. Alec's ears went blank as the bolts detonated.

With a cry of rage, Maimunah jerked her left hand out of Alec's and loosed such a two-handed salvo at Jujuru that the green djinn was hurled half a mile, twisting and gyrating through space. Maimunah's laughter mocked him.

"You think it's a child's game, Jujuru. Wait a moment and I'll show you."

But Alec had no chance to appreciate what Maimunah was about to do to her old foe.

For he was falling, falling like a stone. The sea below swept up and, with a great splash, in he went.

Chapter Thirteen

Alec floated, not on air, but on water. It lapped round his toes and nuzzled his hair with quiet sucking sounds. His arms were folded on his chest, and his body, borne on an invisible current, drifted slowly but steadily along.

Above him the great blue arch of the sky was empty and silent. Either Maimunah and Jujuru had shot each other down or one had destroyed the other, done a victory roll and flown back to base.

Below him, the vast green-blue vault of the sea descended to invisibility. There were moving shadows there, but he could not summon up the energy to guess what they were or if they were interested in him.

His feeling was of infinite pleasure, not the excitement of flying but the contentment of effortless movement. He could float like this for ever. Time stood still. He did not even have the will to look at his watch.

El Samit had told him "If it is written in your destiny . . ." and now he began to understand. If it was written that he should get back his bed, fly to Mahgrib, haul Abu Salem up from the seabed, defeat his enemies (whoever they were) and rescue him from destruction, then that is what he would do. If not, open another door. That was another story.

If not? His mind turned to Eulalia and the club on the coach trip to Blackpool. Sun, sand, sea, food, fun and white knuckles. Well, he was having all that, wasn't he, plus the odd moment of total degradation. Still, that was life.

He pictured the coach hurtling north on the M6 and heard the songs, "Crazy for yoooooooooo!" There was Eulalia – he could see her from the back, head on one side, an arm stretched out, hugging someone's shoulders.

Whose? He did not want to see. Not Ronnie Carter with a fat smirk on his face. Eat your heart out, Bowden! Drown!

Suddenly he was sinking. The sea was reaching round him, over chest, arms, chin, lips, into his mouth. He spluttered, thrashed his arms. He was going down, down, down, into the blue-green yonder and he did not want to go. Destiny be blowed. He demanded a recount.

Darkness flooded his being.

Someone was talking close by, and talking about him, some Reception Committee for Up There, or Down There perhaps.

"He has died young."

"From where did he come?"

"Sheikh, he fell from the skies."

"Allah makes all possible."

"Magic? Is he ins or djinn, man or spirit?"

"He is flesh and bone, though thin."

"The strange bracelet on his wrist, the vessel round his neck."

"Ya. Great value. And by the rules it must be shared."

"O Mahmud, you are the son of vultures."

Alec judged it time to join the conversation. If this was the Reception Committee, he definitely wanted a second opinion.

He opened his eyes. Voices burst around him.

"He lives!"

"A miracle."

"Give him to drink."

A strong arm lifted his head. A metal rim pressed into his lips and cool liquid flowed down his throat. He coughed and sat up.

He was lying on the deck planks of a ship. The rough dark faces of the crew, stripped to the waist, looked down on him. Behind them he saw another figure, tall, slim, elegantly robed in red and green, a young, thoughtful, shy face. He spoke.

"Allah is good. Welcome among us, O Stranger. I am Badr El Din, merchant of Al Basrah, homeward bound with copper, crystal, silk, porcelain, sandalwood, ivory, ebony, mother of pearl, coral, carnelian, brocade, ostrich feathers . . ."

He broke off apologetically. "Not for nothing do people say I am a born merchant. I think and speak of nothing but goods, freight, bills of lading,

102

fifty per cent returns. None is more skilful than I at buying and selling, none is more boring in company. Forgive me."

Helped by the sailors, Alec struggled to his feet. He bowed.

"O most magnanimous of merchants, I owe you my life. I am in your hands. Yet I am of the Children of Adam and no djinn.

"Your servant is a traveller whose ship has sunk and his name is Al Akbar Din." Alec pronounced this with care and was rewarded. No one laughed.

"Shipwreck, O traveller?" The captain's voice and eyes were shrewd and suspicious. "Our helmsman says there were great noises in the heavens and that you fell into the sea."

Alec's mind whirled like a top. What could he say? There was only one thing to do.

He bowed to captain and merchant alike.

"If it is permitted, I will explain. But it is a long story."

At the magic word all sank to the deck, seating themselves around Alec. The captain snapped his fingers and in seconds a boy came running with a brass tray, coffee pot and cups.

Alec thought rapidly. If he told them what had happened that would only make the crew afraid and suspicious of him. What to say? Suddenly he had an inspiration. Out of his memory he borrowed from the Arabian Nights – Sinbad's voyages.

"Your servant is an orphan," he began cunningly, "from Mosul. My small inheritance I invested in goods. I set sail from Al Basrah, bound for the Indies. On the twelfth day from port, we spied a small island.

"Being tired of voyaging, the captain agreed to heave to and some of us landed, meaning to cook and eat a meal and stretch our legs. While some lit fires I went to see if I could find fresh fruit.

"Suddenly, the island shook as if in an earthquake. From the ship the captain called in alarm: 'Come aboard if you value your lives. This is no island but a sea creature who has lived so long it has grown grass on its back. Come or you are doomed.'

"Too late, the monster dived, we were thrown into the sea. The ship raised anchor and sailed away. When the sea calmed, I was alone, clinging to a piece of wood, which Providence put in my way."

The coffee cups were cleared, food was brought. Alec told on, remembering what he could from the Arabian Nights, inventing when memory failed.

At last he came to: "I was carried away by a giant bird, but this in its turn was attacked by others, forced to loosen its grip and drop me from its claws. I fell into the sea, from where my destiny and your kindness saved me."

There was a silence, then the circle of grave listening faces broke into lively chatter, hand clapping, smiles and nods.

"O Akbar Din," said the young merchant, "you have lost your goods, but for that one tale I would replace them ten-fold from my store."

He raised a hand.

"Fear not. I have enough and more. You shall be my guest. Come, you shall sleep in my cabin."

Alec slept into the next day. As he woke he saw Badr El Din busy writing at a table. The young merchant looked up and smiled shyly.

"I trust you slept well. If you permit, I have set down your tale."

"I am honoured."

"The honour is to me." Badr El Din called for food and, as they ate, explained:

"I am a shy and lonely man, though rich beyond the fear of envy. My friends are good to me but I will be honest. They shrink from dining with me, though my table is the richest and most tasteful in Al Basrah.

"As soon as the meal begins I start to talk about goods and prices, markets and such like. The others would like to talk of love and war, of politics, of jests, but I am too shy for women, too timid for fighting, and too innocent for politics. What is more, I have no sense of humour. So I talk of trade until my friends doze at my table.

"Yet now, thanks to our meeting, I have a story to tell which will amaze and delight my guests. Fear not, I shall reward you royally."

"That is not needful," said Alec, hoping Badr El Din would not take him at his word. But his friend leapt up, reached into a chest and pulled out a fat leather bag which jingled as he threw it onto the table.

"A miserable thousand gold pieces. But once we are home in Al Basrah, there will be more."

His shy face had a canny look.

"Has my friend any other stories?"

Alec bowed. "To hear is to serve, O Generous One. I have tales, in all, of seven voyages in the seven seas. But I have one request. That when you tell them, in no way will you use my name. I do not wish that men should think me boastful."

Badr El Din's eyes widened.

"What name shall I write then?"

"Tell them," said Alec, "that you had these stories from a wandering sailor. You could call him Sinbad."

The young man nodded.

"Well said. There is none of that name in Al Basrah. So I shall never be called to account," he chuckled. "My only regret is that my benefactor will not share in the praise which will be heaped on my head. I know that before much time has passed, people will begin to believe, no matter how I protest, that I myself have undergone these trials and adventures."

"Your servant is rewarded enough," said Alec with feeling.

The ship sailed on and, as Alec finished his story-telling, the port of Al Basrah hove into view.

Landing, Alec said farewell to captain and crew and prepared to depart, but his new friend took him by the arm.

"It is selfish to detain you, but I have a reason.

While my goods are unloaded, let us walk about the town to get back our land legs. Then we shall go to my house. You shall be entertained in a manner which will express but a hundredth part of my debt to you and I will make ready for you the payment I promised."

As they walked among the crowded streets and squares of the port, Badr El Din chatted away. Alec wondered how he could ever have been considered shy and tongue-tied. The voyage had loosened him up for sure.

The question was, how soon could he escape the young merchant's hospitality? A sly glance at his watch showed the minute hand past ten thirty. Half his time had gone and he was farther away from Mahgrib than ever.

But, at that moment, another door opened. They rounded a corner into a crowded space.

"The Thieves' Market," said his host, in distaste. "Let us go elsewhere."

"If my Benefactor permits," said Alec, with great self-control, "I would like to see something here."

He darted forward.

In the centre of the market a sale was going on. A crowd of men bargained loud and furiously over a huge pile of goods. And right at the front, almost under the auctioneer's hammer, was a bed; a battered, untidily covered, but utterly desirable bed.

Not a bed. *The* bed.

Chapter Fourteen

As Alec moved forward eagerly the crowd around the dealer broke into derisive laughter. One called:

"Which tripe-cleaner's hovel did you loot that from, O Abdul? I'll give you five dirhans for the lot as firewood and that's charity."

Abdul? Alec, followed by his friend Badr El Din, pushed their way into the group. Sure enough, standing by the bed, dressed in a garishly striped robe and huge turban, was Abdul, son of Abu Salem, as large as life, and in good form.

"O Sheikhs of Excellence. This bed has been slept on by Sons of Fame throughout the Twenty-One Kingdoms. It was in the harem of Khalid, renowned Wali of Damascus," Abdul looked away, "now sadly taken from us."

"Because he was impaled by order of the Sultan. And if justice were done, so would you be," jeered someone in the crowd. "Twenty dirhans and that is my last word."

Abdul's voice rose in indignation: "Allah open another door for you. Why, the cost of porterage alone . . ."

"I will give you one hundred gold dinars."

The voice, quiet but commanding, silenced all around. Alec turned and saw a little way from him two Badawi, one tall, one squat, swords in belts and burnouses pulled down to cover their faces.

"One hundred and fifty!"

Alec had spoken before he realized it. Abdul bowed to him, his expression blank:

"O Face of Good Omen. An Emir of taste and distinction. The bed has found a worthy owner . . ."

Badr El Din plucked at Alec's arm.

"Good friend, do not waste your money on this driftwood. I will give you six beds infinitely better. I have one at home, made of cedar wood plated with gold."

Alec turned to him. "O Badr El Din, do not, I pray you, stand between me and my fancies. This bed, humble as it is, recalls to me the bed I slept on when my parents were still with me."

"Two hundred!" the Badawi's cut across the buzz of chatter in the crowd.

"Three hundred!"

"Four!"

"Five!"

When the Badawi reached fifteen hundred the crowd was silent in awe of the crazy bidding.

Alec opened his mouth to counter, when he stopped. "I forgot, I have only a thousand." But Badr El Din took his arm.

"Bid! I command you. You shall bid to the limit of my purse. I will not see you beaten. Let us see what this desert rover can do."

"Three thousand!"

"Go on," urged Alec's friend. "You shall have that bed. I shall beggar myself to do it."

"Five thousand!" Alec heard himself gasp. He saw a look of fear on Abdul's face.

Then he turned to Badr El Din and said, "No, this is not right. I cannot waste your money like this."

"Not right?" The young merchant's voice took on a stern note. "Not right to help a friend? Allah is just and my reward will be sure. If I do not help you, I shall deserve the verdict of fate."

The words were barely spoken before the Badawi shouted, his voice showing signs of impatience.

"Ten thousand."

Both bidders began to speak together, shouting one another down. Alec called the numbers, not daring to look at his friend's face, until as they reached –

"One hundred thousand!"

Abdul, face pale, raised a hand to stop the calls. "If this continues we shall have the Guild Master upon us or the Caliph's man will denounce us. I beg you, O Emirs, to settle the matter."

The Badawi spoke first, without looking at Alec.

"If the Worthy One will come aside with me, I have something of importance to say to him which will resolve the matter."

Alec caught a look of anguish from Abdul.

The two Badawi abruptly moved away. Alec followed them, but when Badr El Din started to walk with him he urged him: "Wait for me here. Make sure no man touches my bed."

In a narrow lane beside the square, he saw the two men enter a house. It had once been imposing, now it looked battered and neglected. Inside, the courtyard was empty, windswept, its stone ornaments broken and covered with leaves and dust. Beyond, over broken walls, he could see an overgrown orchard. The two awaited him, heads bent.

He said cautiously: "O Sheikhs, your purpose is unknown to me. But that is my bed and I must have it – my life hangs on it."

The tall Badawi suddenly raised his head. The shawl flew to one side. With a shock Alec recognised the olive-green features, the arched eyebrows – Jujuru.

The voice was courteous.

"Your life, O Worthy Youth, is yours to command. As to the bed, you may keep it. May it bring you happiness."

"I can keep it?" Alec was astounded.

"I will exchange it, and the hundred thousand dinars I offered for it, for the vessel which hangs round your neck."

So that was it. The can.

"That is not for exchange or sale," he said.

The "Badawi" remained calm and polite.

"O Fortunate Youth, you place great value on something of little worth – planks, cotton and duck feathers, a piece of inferior metal in an ugly form. Still. My offer stands."

"No. Both bed and can are mine and I will not give, lend or sell them to anyone."

"Let me persuade you," said the tall man.

"Enough!" the squat man who had been silent suddenly exploded. He turned to Alec a broad face of such ugly malevolence it took his breath away.

"Jujuru," he snarled to his companion, "I am weary of this endless playing of games."

He flung out an arm towards Alec.

Jujuru, alarm in his voice, said:

"No, O Highness, O Infinitely Powerful Dahnash, do not, I beg you . . . it will . . ."

Dahnash? The name turned Alec's stomach to ice.

Dahnash ignored Jujuru. Pointing a rigid green finger at Alec, he rasped:

"O Son of Stupidity, take on the form of thy brother."

Alec was paralysed with fear. But for a second nothing seemed to happen. No shrivelling blast, no agony.

Then something did happen. The top of his body began to bow down till his hands touched his feet. His face swelled and jutted out, his ears stretched. His pyjamas ran up his arms and legs, shrinking to hip and shoulders. Fingers fused together, nails blackened. Hair sprang out on the back of his hand and crawled up his arms. Now he was on all fours and his teeth poked between his lips, while hair burst from the base of his spine.

"What the . . ." he tried to say, but what came out was:

"Hee haw."

For a moment he stood stock still, facing the two men. Dahnash lunged at him and Alec felt the hair on his neck stand on end. Then, as Dahnash's long green fingers reached for the can under Alec's neck, Alec moved so swiftly he astonished even himself.

Like lightning his head shot up, the long teeth snapped together like a trap, almost taking the Prince of Darkness's fingers off. Then, wheeling about on his forelegs, Alec lashed out with the back hooves and heard a satisfying crash as both men staggered and fell to the ground.

In the next instant he had cleared the broken wall at a single leap and was crashing away through the orchard.

Chapter Fifteen

At full gallop Alec came out into the side alley on the farther side of the house, turned instinctively away from the Thieves' Market and fled into the maze of the port's side streets.

Behind, voices yelled.

"Help, O people, help. Our little donkey has escaped. The one with the blue and white saddle cloth. Stop him."

Idlers struggled to their feet and lumbered into his path, but he gave them not a second thought. A snap of the jaws here, a head butt there, up on his hindlegs fore hooves flailing, or lashing out in all directions, he cleared a path before him.

Curses, cries of pain, laughter from those unhurt followed him as he tried to put distance between him and his pursuers. Suddenly he knew two things with great clarity.

One was that Dahnash and Jujuru had to keep on pretending they were Badawi from the desert to the west. The other was that if he could get out into the countryside, he might throw them off.

Sniffing the air, he scented water, turned sharply

east and headed to where he knew the great river ran down into the sea.

As he ran and dodged, twisted and turned, his mind wrestled with one question after another. What were those two jokers after? Why did they want the can? Why did Maimunah want the can?

For it was the can they were after, all of them. The bed was just a blind. And the can had to do with Abu. He knew for certain that he had to keep moving and he had to hold on to the can. How he would reach and rescue Abu he could not say. But he knew now that without the can it would be impossible.

At the river bank, he turned north. Fishermen and boatmen idling at the quays turned to stare. But now no one tried to catch him. The noise behind him died away but he did not slacken his pace.

Paved streets gave way to dirt tracks, houses to fields, paths, irrigation channels, water gleaming among the carpet of green, clumps of sugar cane, olive trees, date palms.

He thundered through a village, dogs snapping at his heels, children shrieking and throwing stones, and out into the country beyond. The sun was well up and suddenly he was thirsty.

The water in the ditches was grey-brown. As Alec Bowden he would not have touched it. What he remembered from biology told him nine and ninety foul diseases swam in the channel. But as a donkey, he slurped it with delight. Perhaps his metabolism could cope with it.

Later he stopped to eat, choosing unerringly the shortest, sweetest, green turf. It tasted good, not enough to turn him vegetarian, but better than he expected.

Then he trotted on, conserving his strength. The sun was going down. He would have to stop soon or he'd blunder into one of the ditches. In a small grove he found a place to sleep, pleading with whoever watched over donkeys not to stir up any snakes, scorpions or worse.

And in the dawn he set out again, scrambling to knees, to hooves as though he'd been doing it since birth. He trotted on all that day, and the next. He tried to keep count of their passing. His watch, lost in the hair of his fetlock, was invisible. But he knew that *that* time was passing, too.

On the third day he found a great meadow, full of donkeys and mules, quietly grazing. He joined them cautiously. At first he was ignored, then a small and rather handsome female came along and rubbed noses, followed by a larger, ugly one who was very obviously male. Alec moved off smartly. He found a grazing patch on the side of the herd farthest from the road, and settled down.

He was resting in the shade of the palms and thinking there could be worse lives, when the peace of the meadow was broken.

A series of savage yells sounded on all sides and into the meadow thundered two score horsemen, fiercely bearded.

The herd scattered, but the horsemen were too

116

quick and tightened their circle. From the galloping ring, Alec heard the all-too familiar howl of triumph.

"It is I, El Jawan. Nothing can stand against me, neither king nor prince nor caliph. Nothing can destroy me, sword, lance, noose nor impaling stake. I am El Jawan."

The robbers drove the herd to their camp a dozen miles away, hobbled the donkeys and mules and spent most of the night in drunken revelry. When did they sleep? wondered Alec.

Next day, each beast was loaded almost to dropping with booty from the robbers' raids and the whole procession got on the road.

Alec and his companions were kicked and beaten, flicked with whips and jabbed with goads. He bore all this, as did the others, though he found the language of El Jawan and his comrades a bit much – remarks about his habits, his mother and his sister, where his father had come from. He brooded darkly and waited. Maybe Destiny would come up with something.

The troop halted and they were fed out of evil-smelling bags. The diet was beans, not alas the baked beans which Alec knew and loved, but uncooked. He did not like them and he was sure his fellows did not. But it was all they got apart from the insults and the beatings.

Nose to tail, like heavy traffic on a motorway, they made their way north, snorting and stumbling, backs breaking under their load, until in late afternoon the band entered a thick wood. Twigs and branches crackled underfoot, but the going was softer. Alec felt the journey was nearly over.

It ended by a small hill with a tree on top. Robbers and pack animals crowded together in front of a sheer rock face. Then to Alec's utter astonishment, El Jawan dismounted and shouted:

"Open Sesame."

Suddenly he knew what was going to happen. These were the Forty Thieves from the Arabian Nights. While his mind raced ahead, the robbers were unloading and stacking their booty in the great rock cavern.

But a surprise was coming. When the robbers came to him and pulled the load from his back, one spoke.

"O Chief. See this. This son of a mismatch has a gold cord round his neck."

"I'll have that."

El Jawan was there, shouldering the others aside, reaching out. The sight of his fingernails was enough to put off any self-respecting ass.

There was a tug at the cord. Alec could wait no longer. His long molars clamped tight across El Jawan's wrist and a howl of pure agony rose to the tree tops. From the corner of his eye, Alec saw another robber draw his scimitar. He spun on his forelegs like a ballet dancer, scything with his back hooves. Behind him he heard crunching sounds, grunts, cries of pain.

Circling round, Alec charged, rose up on two legs and flailed like a boxer. Two more went down before him.

What happened next was due to the low cunning of which only a donkey is capable. Alec turned aside and bit another animal. It reared and shouldered a third. In seconds there was a stampede, with men and beasts trapped in a small space. Donkeys lashed out, either in self defence or pure malice. Panicking, the robbers ran into each other. Alec saw one swing with his sword, miss a donkey and strike down one of his fellows.

But he waited for no more treats. He was away, dodging among the bushes and under low trees. No one followed him. He was free again and running.

Chapter Sixteen

He was running. But where? He had no idea. He blundered on, crashing through undergrowth, struggling in thorn bushes until he was worn out and had to stop and rest.

At last when the light was beginning to go he came clear of the forest and saw the winking lights of a small town ahead. A desperate weariness caught up with him as he reached the first houses and he slowed down to walking pace.

Dogs barked, but he did not care. He staggered on, then stopped as he caught, like the finest scent, the smell of ass dung.

He turned into a courtyard. A middle-aged man was closing the gate.

"Why, a gift from Allah. A little donkey. And so weary and worn. O Marjiana, come."

"What is it, O Father Ali?" Ali? Alec shook his head. This must be Ali Baba himself.

A slim dark girl brought a lantern and looked Alec over.

"O Beast of Misfortune, who has beaten you like this?"

She laid a soothing hand on Alec's nose, but

luckily she did not look under his throat. Then she led him away to the stables, shoving the other donkeys aside to make room for him, fed him – beans, of course – and left him.

The next day, when the man Ali came and harnessed Alec together with the other donkeys, Alec had already put in some constructive thinking. It was his destiny to be part of the fate of Ali Baba, was it? Well, maybe he could hurry Destiny up a bit.

They set out for the woods at a leisurely pace. No beating from Ali, though his language left a lot to be desired. Still, the voice was good humoured.

The moment the woodcutter had started work, Alec began to stray. He gave a quiet "hee haw" now and then to draw Ali Baba after him. He could hear him quietly, but less good-humouredly struggling along behind him.

After half an hour they reached the hill and right on cue, Alec's keen ears picked up the sound of hooves in the distance.

Ten minutes later, El Jawan's band reined up before the rock face. By that time, Ali Baba was up a tree and Alec was hiding among the brush.

An hour later, the robbers, having piled in more loot to their cache, had gone away and a mystified and excited Ali was loading Alec and the other donkeys. Alec groaned under the weight of gold and silver bars, and chests of coins and jewels.

Somehow, he had to believe, this must lead him back to his own quest – the rescue of Abu Salem.

The thing was, how and how soon?

It came more quickly than he expected.

Towards dusk they reached Ali Baba's house and clattered into the courtyard.

"Ho, Marjiana, daughter of my soul. Come quickly, help me unload the asses."

There was a bustle, the excited sound of voices. Now Ali's wife was there as well. Bundles, bags and chests were plucked from the donkeys' backs and hurried into the house. The courtyard blazed with lantern light.

It was this light which revealed something vital to Alec. As Marjiana bent over the last of the treasure sacks, something clicked in his mind. He knew that figure. It was not Marjiana the slave girl – it was the person responsible for all – well, most of his troubles – the mischievous girl genie Maimunah.

He did not hesitate but charged full tilt, caught the girl as she bent and sent her flying into the midden. Leaping after her, he butted her down as she tried to rise and thrust her back into the dirt.

She did not scream. She grunted and gasped. Then Alec realized she was laughing, choking with laughter.

"Let me up, O Prince of Beasts," she begged, spluttering with merriment.

Alec stood back. The girl rose, stood hands on hips, then said:

"Revenge is sweet, O Al Ek. But enough is enough."

"When you've re-converted me, you mean. And answered a few questions."

122

Alec forgot all his Arabian courtesies. Not that it made much odds. It all came out in short sharp brays.

And, anyway, Maimunah understood. She raised a hand.

"In the name of Ibn Jann, I conjure you, O Ass. If thou art a beast remain a beast. If thou art a man take thy real form."

Alec felt his forelegs shrink back. He stood upright, ears retracting, face flattening. The hair vanished from arms and legs. The pyjamas slowly slid back to their original position. He was Bowden once more.

He looked quickly at his watch.

It was a quarter to eleven.

Maimunah crooked her finger.

"O Youth of Fair Countenance. Come to my room."

"Oh no," muttered Alec. "No more messing about."

Maimunah shook her head smilingly.

"Be it upon my head and before your eyes. This is needful."

She led him swiftly to a little chamber over the kitchen. Below he could hear the excited whispering of Ali Baba and his wife as they counted the treasure.

By the light of an oil lamp he saw a small bed. But not any bed. This was *the* bed, all right.

He faced the djinniah.

"What is the meaning of all this? I am called to help, to save my old friend Abu Salem. You and this djinn Jujuru – and his evil-tempered comrade Dahnash . . ."

123

"You met Dahnash – and lived?" she breathed.

"I nearly bit his hand off. I certainly gave him one in the chops with my back feet."

She shook her head in awe.

"You have suffered, O Al Ek."

"The truth. I have been abused, humiliated, nearly killed. And you, on purpose, let me fall into the sea. Why, O Maimunah, why?"

"O Unfortunate, but Brave Al Ek. It was all for the vessel that hangs at thy neck. Abu Salem is the last servant djinn, your vessel the last which can command a djinn, and you the last master of a djinn among the Children of Adam. Therefore the vessel cannot be taken from you. You must be persuaded to give it up.

"Jujuru has been trying to get it. I have been trying to prevent him."

"But why?"

"For the sake of the Triumph of Truth, Light and the Good, for the frustration of Evil in the Seven Worlds."

Alec laughed, unpleasantly.

"The Good? And which side are you on?"

She looked at him a moment, in reproach.

"Alas, Al Ek, if only we had known you better. We thought it right – in the name of Good – to keep you safe, that you should know nothing. A little knowledge is a great danger . . ."

"And to be ignorant is to be wise?"

She shook her head, seriously.

"There is much to explain. The Truth should not

be hidden, in the name of the Right. Good cannot be saved by deceit. Now it is too late to explain. Time, our time, your time, djinn time, ins time, is running from us."

She came closer and laid a hand on the cord round Alec's neck.

"You must complete your quest, find Abu Salem and face what will come after. It is fruitless to seek any more to bend the ways of Destiny."

"What will come after?"

"You shall see. Now you must go."

"Very well," said Alec, removing her fingers from the cord round his neck, but unable to resist holding on to them. "One question. If you are on the side of good, what will you do about El Jawan? While Jujuru and you have fought your way across the Twenty-One Kingdoms, El Jawan has killed and plundered. No one seems able to stop him."

"Fear not. His time is nearly come. I shall stay here to protect Ali Baba and his wife. It is written that El Jawan and the robbers shall be destroyed – boiled in oil."

Alec nodded. The fate of the robbers was horrible to think about. But somehow, now, it didn't upset him.

Maimunah lifted up a bag and placed it on the bed. It clinked. Alec guessed it was from the treasure. Then she kissed him, a sisterly kiss.

"Shall we meet again?" he asked her.

"If it is willed." She raised her hand. "O Al Akbar Din. Your destiny awaits."

Chapter Seventeen

As the golden shores of the Secret Sea of Mahgrib came into view, so the can began to crackle.

It was Abdul, who else?

"Hey, Alec, we're in luck. I found Dad."

"Is he all right?" demanded Alec anxiously.

"How should I know? He's still 'en bouteille', ten fathoms down at least. Come in, I'll show you."

"Where are you?" Alec tried to forget all his previous annoyance with the Son of Abu and concentrate on what really counted – releasing the Third Class Genie.

"Headland in the shape of a man's head. Got it? Then little bay, pile of rocks in middle. Right?"

"Got you," said Alec tersely, and put the bed into a long glide that took him over the headland and down to rest on a fine curving beach. What a place, he thought, as he clambered off on to the sand. I bet in our time it's been turned into a villa paradise.

Abdul emerged from among the rocks and took in the look on Alec's face. He raised both hands in a gesture of surrender.

"OK, OK, Alec. One day you'll really appreciate what I've done for you. Got the dosh?"

Alec stared, baffled for a second. Then he held up the bag Maimunah had given him. "I've got – something – here. But what do we want money for?"

"You'll see."

Abdul pointed to the little circle of rocks a little way into the water. A thin, dark man, half naked and bent double, was at work.

"Fisherman," went on Abdul. "If you want to fish up a genie bottle, you need a fisherman. You understand," he added pompously. "All along this coast, rebel genies are banged up in bottles and lying on the seabed for eternity, courtesy of Suleiman the Great."

"For eternity?" Alec was aghast.

"Suleiman the Great never messed about. You don't get to be a world leader otherwise."

"You mean Abu's down there for ever."

"Unless you fish him up – or get him," Abdul pointed to the fisherman, "to haul him up. But it's going to cost."

He saw Alec was still puzzled: "Hauling up djinn is a risky business, Alec. Suppose you, like, get one in your net by chance. You open up and the djinn, feeling angry like with being in solitary since the dawn of time, takes it out on you. So there aren't many fishers who'll take the risk. And those who do, it's strictly a cash transaction."

Alec nodded, which Abdul took to be both understanding and go ahead. Cupping his hands, he shouted:

"O Worthy Fisherman. Would you do a small service for a stranger? Allah rewards all generosity."

The answer was prompt:

"Son of a Dog, leave me in peace. I've caught nothing since dawn. Begone, out of my sight, Face of Ill Omen."

"It is permitted, O Father of a Hundred Good Deeds. Will you make a cast for my good friend?"

"Son of a thousand shameless pigs. If I come and smite you, your length will be your breadth. Leave me alone."

Alec looked skywards, then turned to Abdul.

"Let me try." He waved and shouted to the fisherman.

"O Face of Good Omen. I will pay you a hundred gold pieces for a cast."

The fisherman hauled on his nets and, throwing them over his shoulder, splashed his way to the beach. As he came closer he was a terrifying figure, with his wiry strength, his wild look and filthy clothes. He glared at Alec.

"O Son of Shame. Show me the money."

In his eagerness, Alec opened the bag. At the sight of the gold and silver bars, strings of pearls, gold pieces and jewels, the man's eyes lit up. Then he looked cunning.

"What fish would the Emir have me catch?"

"No fish. At the bottom of the sea lies a flask which I have need of. Cast and bring that up for me, you shall not be disappointed."

"Oho, have I the face of a newborn babe? What

do you take me for? Haul out a cask with a mighty, evil-tempered djinn and be turned into a worm – for a miserable hundred gold pieces."

"Two hundred then."

The fisherman cupped his hands to his ear. "My lord must speak louder. I have salt water in my ears."

"Three hundred."

"A thousand pardons, the sea birds call so loudly and the wind blows your words away."

"Five hundred."

The fisherman bowed low: "May the blessings of Allah spread over you and yours."

Turning to the water, he moved along the edge until he found the place he was seeking. Then, muscles rippling, he whirled the net over his shoulder and cast with a splash that sent ripples spreading across the bay's calm surface.

After a while, he hauled on the net. It came up with fish, seaweed, stones, bits of wood. But no flask.

He turned to Alec. "Alas, luck is not with me today. I cannot think what can be wrong."

"O Father of Lies," burst out Abdul. "Cast deeper."

The fisherman turned, his brow dark, and moved as though to come towards Abdul, then changed his mind. Looking at Alec, he said:

"Place the payment for my first cast on the shore where I can see it. Then I will make another cast, this time for a thousand gold pieces."

Alec winced, then did as he was bid.

"A thousand, when I see the flask."

The fisherman shrugged, then threw his net. After ten minutes, he drew it up, heaving, straining and cursing at the weight. A gruesome dark shape showed through the mesh.

"I am accursed. Or more likely you are," bellowed the fisherman. "A dead donkey."

"Then cast again. My offer was a thousand for the flask."

The fisherman looked cunning. "I did not say I agreed. But charity is noble. I will make a third cast – for the rest of your bag's contents."

"O spawn of the Far One," Abdul danced up and down in rage. "You have been sent to plague us."

The fisherman threw down his nets. "My life is full of woe and weariness. Why should I cast my nets? The rewards are miserable. Go, find another fisherman who will be so patient and kind."

Alec looked at the fisherman, then at his bag, and sighed. Ah well, easy come, easy go, he thought.

He bent down and picked up from the treasure a little pair of earrings, which sparkled red and gold. They made him think suddenly and confusingly about Maimunah and Eulalia. He tucked them into his pyjama pocket. Then he walked along the shore and threw the bag down.

"Cast now, O Fisherman and give me the flask."

The fisherman bowed. "It shall be."

He cast and they waited. And waited. A cool breeze ran along the shore. For some reason, Alec shivered.

130

The water heaved and the net rose into view. As it ran to the shore, Abdul let out a yell.

"There it is, man."

It lay on the shore, round, brown, with a multi-coloured seal. Abdul bent and examined the elaborate inscription.

"That's it, man. Abu Salem, it says."

Picking up the bag and treasure, the fisherman bowed low. "O Sheikh of Munificence, may the dew of blessing fall upon you." Then, throwing his net on one side, he began to dance across the sand, howling and singing in a cracked voice, until he was out of sight.

Alec turned to Abdul. "OK, let's get it open. I don't know how long we've got before – other people arrive."

"Not long, man," agreed Abdul, and, kneeling down, he wrenched at the seal. It flew off with a crack and a rush of air that swelled to a small thunder clap.

Then, there stood Abu, broad-shouldered, turbaned and sashed, his familiar broad face and brown eyes looking bemused, troubled even. Alec had a sudden rush of alarm. There was something wrong here. No smile of welcome, of relief at getting free. Why?

Abu gave him a mournful glance.

"O Evil Day, O Unfortunate Abu Salem."

"Salaam Aleikum, O Abu Salem," Alec spoke quickly, uneasily. "Keef Haalek?"

"Ilhamdulillah," muttered Abu distractedly. Then

131

he turned to Abdul and his voice changed, became stronger.

"It is your fault, O Disobedient One. Did I not always warn you to leave well alone?"

Abdul's eyes rolled.

"Man. Now that is unfair. It was I, O Father, who brought Alec here. It was I, O Alec, who found your bed and safeguarded it, not once but thrice. I brought you together. O truly, the just must wait for their reward."

Alec ignored him. Turning a puzzled face to Abu Salem he said, "But Abu, I heard you call, many times for help. So I came."

Abu pointed to his son.

"It was he, using his father's voice, who did that. O wickedness. O foolishness. Which is worse? Only once did I call thee O Alec, when he," Abu nodded at Abdul, "was in danger of being cut to pieces – deservedly – by El Jawan's men. My feelings as a father triumphed over my good sense."

Abdul turned to Alec. "That's just great, isn't it? You try to help . . ."

Abu shook his head. "Good Intentions are often shaped in Hell." Then he went on in a lower voice. "Tell Alec who asked you to use my voice and call for help. Tell!"

Abdul looked embarrassed, then said, "Jujuru."

"What? Why?"

"Well," Abdul shrugged again. "I owed him one. He covered up for me once or twice. But look, man, it sounded right. There was Dad banged up, and for nothing." He looked sadly at his father. "He is the most honest, do-gooding idiot who ever walked the Seven Worlds. Why should he be locked up?"

"But why all this faking?" asked Alec.

"The can, O Alec," said Abu. "If they could persuade you to give it up, then Jujuru and his Master Dahnash would triumph. They guessed that if they brought you here and threatened me with destruction, you would surrender."

"I'd do anything to help you, it's true."

"I know," returned Abu warmly, "and I could not allow it. You must not surrender the can. I will go down to eternal torment rather than allow that."

"It's no good, Dad," said Abdul. "They are going to get that can. Nothing will stop them."

"You think so," answered Abu angrily. "Your generation which pretends to believe nothing will accept anything."

Alec said slowly. "So you were not imprisoned? You were hidden. And I was deceived. What a mess."

Abu nodded: "The Great Ibn Jann asked me to hide. Under the seal of Suleiman, even Dahnash himself could not touch me."

Abdul stared: "You mean, O Father, they would have left you in there for ever, just to put one over Dahnash?" He snorted: "Some Goodness. Some Truth."

Abu shrugged: "Some things your generation will never understand."

"Well," said Alec, as cheerfully as he could. "I've got the can. They won't get it from me."

"O Alec, you do not know what they can do. You have not crossed their path."

Alec laughed: "O but I have. I've met Jujuru and Dahnash as well."

"And you lived to tell, O Alec? O Miracle."

"Look," Alec became decisive. "We've got the bed. Let's move. Point is, where do we go?"

Abu spoke thoughtfully: "There may be a chance light enough to ride on a hair. There will be a little time before they know I am out of the flask. It may be enough to reach Djinnistan and take refuge with Ibn Jann."

"So," said Abdul, "what are we waiting for?"

Chapter Eighteen

The bed soared away. Alec's anxiety for Abu's safety seemed to give it extra power. The speed was dizzying, and below them desert, oasis, mountains, lakes, rivers, forests, more mountains and sand, sand, sand, passed in a blur.

"I have often thought of you, O Alec," said Abu, "of the lovely Eulalia and the pugnacious Ginger, the evil Denny and the woeful Spotty Sam. But never did I think we would meet again like this. O Alec, Unhappy Day that I, who wished only to serve you, should put your life in peril."

"Abu," Alec returned more firmly than he felt, "I wanted to come. Nobody could make me. Nobody could keep me away. And nobody's going to stop me now."

He felt the bed shake and creak beneath him as the speed increased.

"How much further? I'm not sure the bed won't shake itself to pieces before we get there."

Abu looked ahead keenly, then pointed.

"Do you see those hills beyond the wide empty plain? Those green hills are the borders of Djinnistan. Once among them we are safe."

"Right. So fasten your seat belts. I am coming in to land – now."

Alec put the bed into a long glide. The green hills grew larger, more distinct, closer with every second.

Then, quite suddenly, they had vanished. In their place was an emptiness, a dazzling whiteness. The bed stopped in mid-air and then slowly, irresistibly, began to sink to the ground. Nothing Alec could do could keep it airborne. They went down, down, down.

And at last it rested on the ground. Ahead to left to right, behind them, was blank whiteness.

"What's happening, Abu?" cried Alec.

"The worst, I fear."

"And the worst is the best, of course," said a mocking voice from beyond the white screen.

"Jujuru!" all three spoke at once.

"The same, O Youth of Excellent Intention but too Little Understanding. All flight is impossible. You are in my hands. It is time to end this game, time for you to surrender."

As Jujuru spoke, the whiteness vanished.

In its place, walls began to form, in a perfect circle around them. They were in a small circular room, like the top of a lighthouse. It had one window, yet it did not look out on anything.

Instead, the window space was filled with the handsome, mocking green face of Jujuru, dark curving eyebrows raised as he looked in on them.

"This slave's house is yours," he said. "Your comfort is my only thought."

He looked at them keenly.

"You are shivering. Is the house too cold?"

In the next instant heat from hell seemed to fill the room, bathing them with sweat and sending hands clutching at throats.

"Water," gasped Abdul.

"Hearing is obeying," said Jujuru.

There on a table in front of them was a bowl of water. Abdul seized it and began to pour water into his mouth then howled as his face and head were suddenly wreathed with coiling snakes.

"You are perspiring. I fear it is a little too warm." Jujuru's voice was reassuring in its politeness.

Cold blasted into the tiny space, the walls dripped with ice and the window frame sparkled with frost. It struck through their thin clothes and set them dancing in pain.

Alec gritted his teeth and forced himself to meet Jujuru's gaze.

"My five fingers in your left eye, my five fingers in your right," he gasped.

There was a look of surprise, and alarm in Jujuru's eyes. He flinched. The face faded from the window and the room returned to its first state.

Jujuru's voice came through faintly but clearly.

"As you wish. I will wait. I have time, if you have not."

Now they were left in silence. The three looked at one another helplessly. It seemed to Alec that he could hear his watch ticking. The second hand appeared to pick up speed.

But that must be an illusion. Time had no meaning any more. They were here for eternity or until he gave in. He looked at Abu, then at Abdul, but they did not return his glance.

He thought of Eulalia. He would not see her, nor anyone else at home, Mum, Dad, Kim, Granddad, no one. He would just vanish, cease to exist. That's what it meant. And yet one word from him and it would be over. Just that Abu and Abdul . . .

The thought of Eulalia made him feel in his pocket for the red-gold earrings he had taken from the bag. All the rest of the treasure had gone to that foul-mouthed fisherman. Well, much good may it do him, he thought. It's not done me any good.

He pushed the earrings back. Might as well keep them, as a souvenir of – everything.

As he did so, his fingers touched something prickly.

He jerked the fingers out and stared. There was the tuft of hair El Samit, the ghoul-marid, had given him – when was it? Years ago. Or was it at quarter past ten?

He held it up and turned to Abu.

"One last spell, O Abu Salem, if you will?"

Abu looked curiously at the hair. "Hearing is Obeying, O Alec."

"Set this alight for me."

Abu took the hair and placed it on his palm. He muttered briefly over the tuft and then with a puff of smoke and sparks it burst into flame. And was gone.

Nothing happened. Was that it? Alec shrugged. There was nothing more to be done, then.

"Hey, man," said Abdul, "what's with this place? The joint is jumping."

The whole tower had begun to rock as if in a hurricane. It shook violently. Cracks opened in ceiling and wall. Sky and sun shone through. Gaps widened and with a great crash the whole mass of stone collapsed.

El Samit, giant-like, hairy, bleary-eyed, stood there.

"O Excellent Youth, what has brought you to this pass?" he bellowed.

"It is a long story, O El Samit. But accept my grateful thanks."

"It is well," answered the ghoul-marid, and with a great blast like escaping steam he vanished.

They stood now by the bed in the plain where they had landed. Ahead of them, seemingly only a little distance from them, were the green hills of Djinnistan.

"Come on. Jump aboard," shouted Alec. The others, still bewildered, obeyed. But the bed would not move.

Alec leapt off in disgust.

"Let's run for it."

But as they ran, the mountains vanished. Before them, on the great expanse of the plain, appeared a huge row of pillars, gleaming a ghastly green, like rotten teeth.

Above them from the pillars reached out a vast

roof extending over their heads and far beyond. Alec looked back. More pillars and walls were growing out of the soil, green, glistening with poisonous dew.

Around them rose a babel of terrible sounds, shrieks, moans, foul laughter, snarls of vicious rage.

To their left, and behind them appeared an army of grotesque creatures, winged and scaled, stamping and writhing dragon-like, snake-like, vulture-like. Their voices rose to an ear-splitting din.

In front of them rose up a great dais with a throne cut from ghastly white bone. Before it stood a table made from a great single piece of jade.

"O Evil Day," said Abu. "All is lost. This is the flying palace of Dahnash, Prince of Darkness, come from beneath the Sea of Eternity, from which no one escapes."

Chapter Nineteen

As Abu spoke, the massed ranks of fiend-dom rose to their feet, tails and wing-tips, and let loose a shout of triumph that made the pillars quiver. On the throne, wrapped in a robe of nauseous purple, appeared the squat green curly-haired figure of Dahnash. At his side, arrogant and deferential at the same time, was Jujuru.

"Hail to the Prince of Darkness. Victory to Evil. Abomination triumph!" they yowled.

Dahnash rose. There was a silence so utter that Alec thought he could hear the slime drip down the columns. From behind the throne advanced two winged djinns, massive shoulders bowed under the weight of something round, which they placed on the jade table. Their job completed, they left.

Alec stared. It was a great ball of metal, dull grey in colour and rough edged. He turned in bewilderment to Abu. But Abu placed a finger to his lips. Jujuru had advanced to the front of the dais.

"O Mighty Dahnash, Supreme Inspirer of Every Evil Thought and Deed within the Seven Worlds, the moment of your triumph is at hand."

Dahnash turned this way and that. To Alec that smile had all the self-satisfaction of a seven-year-old who has just nicked a slice of cake and got away with it. That made his stomach grow cold.

Jujuru continued:

"What others failed to do, you accomplished. Here in this ball lies all the metal of all the magic objects to which all the Djinn of Suleiman the Great were enslaved by the Oath of Obedience. And now it is in your hands."

Another howl of triumph, then silence.

"All that remains is one fragment to complete the sum, an insignificant twenty grammes of base metal. That alone stands between you and the command of every spirit in the universe whether that spirit is devoted and loyal to the noble Cause of Infamy, or whether it sneaks and crawls around the worlds forcing its good deeds upon unhappy creatures."

The assembly let go its breath in a long whistle of contempt.

"And now," Jujuru leapt from the dais and strode down the hall, "that miserable piece of metal which we lack is within our grasp."

The chilling eyes of every fiend followed him until they rested on Alec.

"Here," Jujuru's hand rested lightly on the cord round Alec's neck. "Here it is."

The din was incredible and with it came a great wave of fetid odour from the overheated crowd. It made Alec choke. But he swallowed and found his voice. In the still that followed he heard it echo under the vaulted roof.

"O Jujuru, Slave of Disgust and Abysmal Cunning and the Infinitely Degraded Son of a Mismatch whom you serve."

To his scared delight he saw Dahnash start from his throne, while the great rout gazed in awe as if they did not believe their eyes and ears. The Prince of Darkness insulted in his own palace. But Dahnash controlled himself.

Jujuru's face close to Alec's was impassive, though it seemed to him that there was a gleam of something mysterious in those narrowed eyes. Jujuru spoke:

"O Al Ek Bahdeen, he who comes late." He waited for the jeering laughter to die down. "You are one of the Children of Adam and the time of your destruction is not yet come. Thus the insults you heap on us, the breath you take while you speak, are gifts from us. You may say what you will. It will serve no purpose except to waste the time which is precious to you."

In spite of himself Alec looked at his watch. The second hand had crept past ten to eleven. Time was nearly up. But for whom? He found his voice.

"For you, too, O Jujuru and your One-Dirhan Master. You have no more time than I have, you to destroy and I to save."

Jujuru's eyes showed reluctant admiration. "We have enough," he said, quietly, as though Alec and he were chatting by themselves.

"But I will not wait!" Dahnash was on the edge of the dais and roaring. From the hall his words were picked up.

"We-will-not-wait."

Dahnash yelled: "O Worm, give up that vessel which means nothing to you to its rightful owner. I command you!"

"I refuse," answered Alec, and heard a low groan from Abu Salem.

The djinns who had brought in the metal ball suddenly reappeared, striding down the hall. Without a word they dragged Abu, to snarls of glee from the ranks of fiends, and threw him to the floor before the throne.

To see his old friend and helper, so strong, so wise, so good and brave, helpless and humiliated like this turned Alec's guts to water. Suddenly, now, he was afraid, because he knew that the time for being helped was over. Now he had to do the helping, the protecting. If there was any magic he had to make it.

Snatching the can from round his neck, he marched to the dais, stepping between the prostrate Abu and the throne. He raised the can, but as Dahnash reached out a green arm to snatch it, he held it away.

Then turning and facing east, he raised the can higher, above his head and shouted.

"O Ibn Jann, King of Djinnistan, I will stay faithful to the Djinn of the Can, Abu Salem, no matter what may be. I will do what is needful, but do not thou, O Ibn Jann, abandon thy servant."

144

He paused in the eerie silence.

"If you desert him in his hour of need, I swear I will hand over this can to Dahnash, Prince of Darkness, at the count of seven."

Silence again, as Alec began to count.

And on the seventh number, there came a clap of thunder that shook the green palace.

The pillared hall to the east fell away, light poured in and, as the dust settled, extending away into the distance, another palace appeared, pillared and arched like the first, but in red and gold.

Its floor was packed with ranks of Djinn in the form of men, women and animals of every kind and on its dais, magnificent in his robes, sat Djinnistan's king, and by his side, tall, handsome as ever, but unsmiling, stood Maimunah.

Chapter Twenty

Cheers and counter cheers crashed out, rebounding from the roofs of the twin palaces.

Ibn Jann rose, ignoring Dahnash but speaking to Alec.

"O Worthy but Impetuous Youth. You have had your wish, to meet your destiny alone. But you cannot decide the issue. This lies beyond your power. There is no shame in this. To everyone must come the time when Higher Powers join battle."

Turning to Dahnash, formal, even courteous, Ibn Jann spoke again:

"O Dahnash, Prince of Darkness. I call on you in the name of Suleiman the Great to desist from this insane quest for Power over the Seven Worlds. It is not to you nor to me or any of our kind. I bid you cease. Release the Djinn Abu Salem and his son Abdul. Let their master return to the Children of Adam to whom he belongs."

Dahnash's chest swelled until he looked like a demented frog. Then the words came storming from his mouth.

"To you, Ibn Jann, and to your Suleiman the Great, I offer my defiance and contempt. Oppose me and pay the price. I stand on the brink of limitless power. Deeds cannot stop me. Words are a waste of breath. Stand in my way and you shall be annihilated. Suleiman the Great, Destroyer of Rajmus, my noble father, is gone. Soon you will join him."

Ibn Jann listened, then raised his hand.

"O Rash Prince, Foolish as you are Evil. I conjure you in the name of the Most High."

At that name a sigh like the wind passed through the twin palaces and, in the hush that followed, Dahnash answered.

"If I feared the Most High who destroyed my Grandfather, I would abandon hope and creep about doing good for the rest of time. But hereby I proclaim my defiance also of Him. If by design or accident I should do one miserable good deed, may I rot away or burn to ashes for eternity."

Now even Dahnash's followers seemed petrified by his recklessness.

"I am tired of waiting," yelled Dahnash.

"Take the worm Abu Salem and destroy him before the eyes of his master. Cut him into pieces and make him eat them one by one."

Alec was seized by nausea. He clenched his hands to control himself and stared helplessly at Maimunah. But she was not looking at him. Her eyes were on Jujuru as he drew his scimitar and advanced on Abu, standing square and firm at Alec's side.

But in the next second, Abu had gone. A tiny

147

movement caught Alec's eye, as a small insect no more than a flea scurried for the shadow of the dais.

Jujuru vanished. Alec jumped as a great hairy spider scuttled across his feet. But just as its jaws snapped over the fleeing insect there was a light thump on the floor nearby.

A lizard, tongue flicking in and out, closed in on the spider. The insect was nowhere to be seen. Neither was Maimunah.

In the flash of a second the spider became a snake. The lizard dodged frantically away then turned into a mongoose, weaving and dodging, to leap at the snake's throat.

Now the snake was a tiger, the mongoose a lion, the tiger an elephant. The changes came so fast they flitted across Alec's vision like a film,

The beasts had gone, the floor was covered in twisting undergrowth. A scythe came from nowhere to mow it down, swinging and slashing. Fire blazed up and swallowed the scythe. Alec heard Jujuru's shout of triumph.

But that was cut short as a torrent of water swept past, snuffing the flames. Black smoke poured from the embers. Now Maimunah's voice pealed out.

"In the name of Ibn Jann, victory is mine."

Flushed and panting, she appeared, bowing low before the King's Throne.

But as she did, Jujuru, breathless but still laughing, faced her. Applause thundered and crackled round the double hall.

As it died away, Alec saw a small movement by the platform. Then Abu Salem was by his side. His brown face was ashen with fear and strain. But he held himself upright.

Ibn Jann spoke.

"Let that be, Dahnash. You cannot prevail."

Maimunah laughed and pointed at Jujuru.

"Perhaps Jujuru would like another trial of strength and cunning. A second time, I promise, I will not let him escape so easily."

Jujuru laughed back. "Only my respect for woman-kind prevented me from plunging you to utter destruction."

"Enough," raged Dahnash. "Time passes. I will not wait. We will make one more test. And if I win, that vessel shall be mine and you, Ibn Jann, must accept the verdict of Destiny."

"What test?" asked the Djinn King.

"Something of absurd simplicity, O Fountain of Goodness," sneered Dahnash. "A game of riddles."

"Riddles," Maimunah's voice was scornful. "To put the fate of the Seven Worlds upon the outcome of a child's game? Why not spin a coin?"

Dahnash chuckled: "Are the Champions of Truth and Light afraid of a child's game? I am not. I shall take part myself."

There was a great buzz from both sides of the twin palace, like a summer rainstorm.

"So be it," said Ibn Jann, reluctantly. "But, if you are defeated, O Prince of Darkness, you will accept defeat, that is clear?"

Dahnash giggled. "There is a condition. Since I am contending for possession of that vessel, then my opponent shall be," he paused for effect, "the one that owns it."

The air filled with laughter, protests, yells and counter shouts. Ibn Jann, outraged, rose to his feet.

But Alec stepped forward.

"I accept. The can is mine. I have the choice."

"O Foolish One," called Maimunah. "You cannot win. He will cheat."

"Are you afraid, O Spirits of Truth?" demanded Dahnash. His voice, vicious yet childish, was chilling. "While time slips by, you have tried by all means in your power to avoid this moment. But now it cannot be delayed any more. The time has come."

Ibn Jann's face was troubled. He looked down at Alec.

"If you accept, we have no choice. Our fate is in your hands."

He mused for a moment.

"From the Dawn of Time, this battle has been fought. And always for the sake of the Children of Adam. So it is right that in this moment you should play your part. Let it be."

A last burst of sound came from the halls and then there was silence once more. Alec saw that Jujuru was now standing close behind the throne. He thought those curved lips were moving.

"I will begin," said Dahnash.

"What grows when it eats and dies when it drinks?"

Alec's brain turned. The riddles he had shared with El Samit, the ghoul-marid, raced through his brain. Without knowing it, he found the answer.

"Fire," the word burst from his lips.

Djinnistan's ranks applauded. Their opponents hissed. All faces turned to Alec.

"What is the most precious thing in the world which all must have?"

"Power," said Dahnash.

"No."

"Money."

"No."

"Rubbish," roared the Prince of Darkness. "Everyone wants money or power!"

"Maybe," said Alec, "but that is not what they need and cannot do without."

Jujuru's lips moved again.

"Sleep, sleep," shouted Dahnash. "All must sleep."

"True," nodded Alec.

"You are cheating, Dahnash. Jujuru told you," called Maimunah.

"If I am," came Jujuru's mocking reply, "it is in my nature."

"What if we help Al Ek, in our turn?"

Jujuru smiled. "You will not. It is not in your nature to cheat. We must fight the battle according to our own ways."

"Let the contest continue," Dahnash was shaking with excitement. "I will ask."

"The tree has twelve branches, each branch has

two clusters, one cluster has thirty white berries, the other thirty black cherries. What is it?"

Alec's mind fused. It went blank. The working parts would not move. This was one he had never heard. He began to look about him, but Jujuru called, ironically, "Do not cheat, O Al Ek, it is not in your nature."

Alec shook his head. "I do not know."

"We have won, we have won," crowed Dahnash. "The answer is a year, month and nights and days."

Ibn Jann rose in wrath. "No. No. The contest is not complete until three riddles have been asked on either side. Ask your second, O Alec."

Alec breathed deeply, gradually the tight feeling between his eyes beginning to ease. He spoke slowly.

"He who bought it did not need it. He who made it could not use it. He who used it did not know it."

There was a hush in the twin palaces. Alec saw Jujuru look puzzled. Dahnash turned towards him, but the lieutenant's lips did not move. Reluctantly, petulantly, Dahnash shook his head.

"I do not know."

They looked at Alec.

"A coffin," he shouted.

A second's pause then a wave of laughter swept the halls. Both sides cheered.

Now began the third round and tension grew in audience and contestants alike.

"What has an eye but cannot see?" asked Dahnash.

"A needle," answered Alec, then asked, "Who meet by night and part by day?"

Dahnash, prompted by Jujuru, answered: "Double doors."

Ibn Jann spoke.

"It is good. The contest is drawn. Acknowledge that you cannot win, Dahnash, and that this youth has played fairly and that, despite cheating, you cannot overcome him. Accept the verdict of the trial."

"No," Dahnash's voice was high and cracked. "Let there be one final riddle to decide."

"But who shall ask it?"

Dahnash looked crafty. "We shall dice!"

Ibn Jann's face was full of suspicion. "Dice?"

"Yes. Maimunah and Jujuru shall throw one throw. The greatest number decides who shall ask." Then he paused, smirking, "And to make sure that the Good do not cheat the Bad, she shall throw for me, and Jujuru will throw for the Youth."

Ibn Jann was troubled, but said. "Very well, bring the dice."

A djinn appeared bearing an embroidered cushion on which rested two large ivory dice.

Jujuru bowed with old-fashioned courtesy. "Cast, Maimunah. You will not cheat. Throw your best throw for your most hated enemy."

Maimunah glared at him, clasped the dice in her hands, muttered to herself and rolled.

"Five and six," intoned the djinn.

No one spoke. No one seemed to breathe as Jujuru took his turn. With a wicked grin he threw.

"Six and six."

As the numbers were called, there was pande-
monium. Dahnash leapt up in fury, glaring at his
lieutenant. But Jujuru shrugged apologetically.

"Even the Prince of Darkness does not control
chance," he said.

Ibn Jann called to Alec.

"Ask, O Youth of Virtue. The Seven Worlds
hang upon your lips."

Alec was silent. The riddles he knew, those he
had learned, went through his mind. One by one he
discarded them. He knew that all those were known
to Jujuru, who would be bound to tell his chief. He
must think up one completely new. He must make
one up. He thought.

"Do you give up?" demanded Dahnash spitefully.

"No!" Alec shouted. Behind him the fiends snig-
gered. But when Alec finally began, they were silent.

"What has no legs but travels swifter than a
horse? What has no body but lives in all cities
at once? What makes us laugh and cry in the same
moment? What costs nothing but enriches all?

"What lasts but a short while but endures
for ever? What is easily forgotten but always
remembered? What tells the truth when it seems
to lie? What takes the poor wife from her cooking
pot and the king from his council chamber? He who
brings it leaves it behind and takes it away with him.
What is it?"

Alec let his breath go. It was finished. He had
done his best and now, he grinned to himself, it's
Destiny's turn.

Dahnash shifted in his seat, turned like a child and looked pleadingly to Jujuru. But Jujuru's green handsome face was blank. Alec exulted in himself. They did not know.

Dahnash jumped up, then slumped in his seat sending out a howl of rage.

"I – do – not – know."

Ibn Jann turned to Alec.

"O Youth, speak. What is the answer?"

"It is simple," said Alec. "In a word, a story."

No cheers, no stamping, no boos, no cries or screams of rage. Nothing. Dahnash tottered to his feet. Jujuru moved to help him but the arm was thrown aside. Slowly the beaten Prince of Darkness walked away from his throne, the green hair hanging lank on his drooping body.

"Wait," called Alec.

Dahnash stopped. All listened.

"It is not enough to walk away. There is the price of defeat."

"What is that?" groaned Dahnash.

"The ball of metal must be destroyed."

"What?" Dahnash squeaked.

"Yes," said Alec, "let there be an end to slavery for djinn. Let them choose what they will serve as free spirits. Let the metal melt into liquid and escape into the air as vapour and disappear."

Ibn Jann raised a hand. The floor opened. From below poured flames. Two djinn took the metal ball and let it fall into the pit. A great cloud flew up and dispersed. Then the pit began to close.

"Wait," Dahnash spat the word. "There is still one piece of metal, is there not?"

He advanced towards Alec, hand outstretched.

"It is right, O Youth," said Ibn Jann. "The last Djinn must be set free, if your words mean anything."

Against his will Alec protested: "That means I'll never see Abu Salem and Abdul again."

Maimunah shook her head. "In dreams, O Al Ek. It is a little loss to bear, after what you have done today."

Alec took off the can and handed it to Dahnash. The pit opened briefly and the can was thrown in. Then the fire vanished.

Dahnash recovered some dignity and faced his troops.

"Take wing, O Wicked Ones. Have no fear. As long as the Children of Adam live there will be work for us to do."

There was a great current of air, an immense clattering of wings, and in a moment all were gone, leaving the djinns of Ibn Jann in possession. Slowly the green palace began to melt and crumble, until it had vanished entirely.

Alec stared. Jujuru was still standing there. He saluted Alec.

"O Youth of Good Omen," he smiled. "I shall miss you as you travel the path of virtue. Promise me that now and then you will lie and cheat a little, so that I may know what you are doing and that you are well." He smiled. "Now farewell – do not think too kindly of me."

Alec laughed: "O Jujuru, you give evil a good name. But one question before you go."

"What is that?"

"Tell me, did you cheat with the dice, to give me a twelve? Did I win by a false throw?"

Jujuru threw back his head and laughed.

"But certainly I cheated. What else? I am always true to myself."

And he was gone.

Alec took his place on the bed. He had said his farewells to Abu Salem and Abdul. Abu hugged him. Abdul punched his shoulder and winked. Now he found himself, as so often, alone with Maimunah. She bent over the bed and kissed him.

"O Youth of Excellence. May the Dew of Blessing fall upon you."

"And on you. O Maid of Virtue, despite all," answered Alec impudently.

She smiled.

"I have a boon to ask."

"It is granted already."

"In your pocket you have two red and gold earrings kept back from Ali Baba's treasure. Give me one as a keepsake."

Alec hesitated, but she held out her hand. He grinned sheepishly and handed one over.

She took it and bowed.

"It is done. Go to meet your Destiny. O Al Akhar Din."

Chapter Twenty-One

"Alec! Alec! ALEC!"

Someone was calling him. With each repetition the voice grew more annoyed.

He sat up. He was in bed, in his room. The journey had gone so swiftly he remembered nothing of it. He looked at his watch. It was five to eleven.

That must be Mum calling. No, it wasn't. She was out today. That was one reason he'd overslept in the first place.

Pebbles clattered on the panes. He staggered to his feet and looked out of the window. In the backyard, looking up, was Eulalia.

"You are the absolute end. In your pyjamas. Come on! Everybody's waiting for you. Get dressed and come on."

"B-but . . ."

"Stop but-butting. Get dressed. You've got five minutes to get down here."

Alec staggered round the room, stripping off pyjamas and pulling on shirt and jeans. Then back to the window.

"Eu. Why am I doing this? Why are you here? It's five to eleven."

"Alec Bowden," she exploded. "Not only do you not know the time of day, or the day of the week, you don't even know the month of the year."

"What d'you mean?"

"It's five to *ten*, you idiot. The clocks went back last night."

"You what?"

Alec was dancing a jig round the room. Now he understood the time bit, why he had an hour, an hour that didn't exist in real time. And in that hour, he'd travelled the Twenty-One Kingdoms, saved Abu Salem, made a monkey of the Prince of Darkness and saved the universe from destruction.

"O Milk-White Day. O Happy Bowden," he yodelled as he threw himself down the stairs. He missed the last three and hit his head on the door, but he barely noticed.

Two minutes later, he was running down the road with Eulalia. As they reached the canal bridge he pulled up.

"Hey, Eu," he said. "You said that if I wasn't there at five to ten you'd give the ticket to Ronnie Carter."

She glared at him, then laughed. "Don't believe everything you hear. If you didn't have a guilty conscience you'd know I would no more sit all the way to Blackpool and back with that prize plonker than I'd walk starkers down the High Street."

He laughed with her, then stopped and fished in his pocket.

"Eu."

He held out the earring, trying to think of a credible way of explaining why there was only one.

But she cut him short with a shriek. She kissed him.

"Magic, Skinny. Where did you find it? I thought it was gone for good. Look!"

From her jeans pocket she pulled out an earring. Red-gold, it was the duplicate of the other.

"Our aim is your delight, O Daughter of Excellence," he said, bowing.

She chuckled.

"Give over, Skinny. Come on. They're starting."